THE MAGNIFICENT MEAULNES

Alain-Fournier was born Henri Alban Fournier, the son of two school teachers, on 3 October 1886 in La Chapelle d'Anguillon in France. He studied at a boarding school in Paris, at the naval college in Brest, and also at the Lycée Lakanal in Sceaux, where he met his lifelong friend, the critic Jacques Rivière. In 1905 Fournier had a chance meeting with Yvonne de Quiévrecourt and fell instantly in love. This meeting was the inspiration for *Le Grand Meaulnes*, though the novel was not finished until Fournier had completed his military service in 1913. While working as a columnist and private tutor, Fournier was called up to fight in the First World War. He was killed in action at Vaux-les-Palameix in 1914, though his body was not formally identified until 1991. *Le Grand Meaulnes* is his only finished novel.

Valerie Lester is the author of *Phiz, The Man Who Drew Dickens* (2004) and *Fasten Your Seat Belts! History and Heroism in the Pan Am Cabin* (1996). She has published essays and poems in various venues including *The Atlantic Monthly, Airways Magazine,* and *The New Dictionary of National Biography*. She first tried translating *Le Grand Meaulnes* as a teenager at school in Switzerland, and finished the job half a century later.

ALAIN-FOURNIER

The Magnificent Meaulnes

TRANSLATED FROM THE FRENCH BY
Valerie Lester

VINTAGE BOOKS
London

Published by Vintage 2009

2 4 6 8 10 9 7 5 3

Translation copyright © Valerie Lester 2009

Le Grand Meaulnes first published in France in 1913

This translation first published in Great Britain by Vintage in 2009

Vintage
Random House, 20 Vauxhall Bridge Road,
London SW1V 2SA

www.vintage-classics.info

Addresses for companies within The Random House Group Limited
can be found at: www.randomhouse.co.uk/offices.htm

The Random House Group Limited Reg. No. 954009

A CIP catalogue record for this book
is available from the British Library

ISBN 9780099529729

The Random House Group Limited supports The Forest Stewardship
Council (FSC), the leading international forest certification
organisation. All our titles that are printed on Greenpeace approved
FSC certified paper carry the FSC logo. Our paper procurement
policy can be found at www.rbooks.co.uk/environment

Printed and bound in Great Britain by
CPI Bookmarque, Croydon CR0 4TD

CONTENTS

THE MAGNIFICENT MEAULNES

TRANSLATOR'S NOTE

A translator of *Le Grand Meaulnes* comes across some sentences that do not easily give up their hold on French. Almost all can eventually be wrestled down, but one in particular remains adamant:

> Quant à Jasmin, qui paraissait revenir à cet instant d'un voyage, et qui s'entretenait à voix basse mais animée avec Mme Pignot, il était évident qu'une cordelière, un col bas et des pantalons-éléphant eussent fait plus sûrement sa conquête.

Frank Davison, in his 1959 translation, takes this stand: 'Meanwhile Jasmin was engaged in lively conversation with Madame Pignot, addressing her in low tones, though one felt that a sailor's red pompom, blue collar, and bell-bottomed trousers would have been more to her taste.'

Robin Buss's 2007 translation reads: 'He was speaking in a low voice, but eagerly, to Madame Pignot, and it was clear that a sailor's piping, low collar and bell-bottomed trousers would have been more to his liking.'

An interpreter friend of mine, Sylvie Battigne, translates the sentence: 'Jasmin was talking in a low but animated voice with Mrs Pignot, and it was obvious that a rope belt, a flat collar and bell-bottom pants would help in her (or his) conquest.' Sylvie hits at the root of the problem and comments, 'I don't know who is trying to conquer whom (Mrs Pignot, Jasmin, or the outfit)'. The ambiguity comes, of course, from the 'sa' of '*sa conquête*', which looks feminine and works on the subliminal to translate it as 'her', but can just as plausibly be 'his'. And Sylvie's mention of the outfit focuses attention on the knotty word 'cordelière'. *Une cordelière* is a Franciscan nun, complete with rope belt, but I don't think any translator would dare translate the phrase: '. . . it was obvious that a Franciscan nun in bell-bottom trousers would have been more to his/her taste.'

I offer Alain-Fournier's puzzle as a challenge to all you translators out there. Personally, I went for 'her' (because of Madame Pignot's alleged amorousness), eschewed red pompoms, and stuck with the rope belt.

The Magnificent
Meaulnes

PART I

CHAPTER I

THE BOARDER

HE arrived at our place on a Sunday in November 189__.

I continue to say 'at our place' even though the building no longer belongs to us. We left the area nearly fifteen years ago and will certainly never return.

We were housed in part of the secondary school at Sainte-Agathe. My father, whom I called Monsieur Seurel just as the other students did, was in charge of the top form, where students worked towards a teacher's diploma. He also taught the middle form. My mother was in charge of the younger students.

Imagine a long, red, vine-covered building with five glass doors, just outside the market town; a huge courtyard, with a covered playground, a wash house, and a large gateway opening towards the village; on the north side, a little gate to the road leading towards the station three kilometres away; on the south side, fields, gardens, and meadows meeting up with suburbs. Now you can see in your mind's eye the place where I spent the dearest but most tormented days of my life – the location from which adventures ebbed and flowed, shattering us like waves on a remote rock.

Fate, in the form of a transfer dreamed up by some inspector or administrator, brought us to Sainte-Agathe a long time ago. We moved there at the end of the summer holidays, in a country wag- gon which preceded the household goods. When it deposited my mother and me in front of a rusty gate, several urchins, busy stealing peaches in the garden, quickly scurried away through gaps in the hedge. My mother, whom we called Millie and who was the most methodical housekeeper I have ever known, bustled into the dusty, hay-strewn rooms, muttering with despair, as she did each time we moved, that our furniture would never look right in such a badly constructed house. She came back outdoors to convey her distress to me while she dabbed gently at my grimy child's face with her handkerchief. Then she returned inside to assess how many openings would have to be bricked up to make the place habitable. As for me, I remained outside on the gravel of the strange courtyard. Still wearing my large, beribboned straw hat, I ferreted around the well and the shed while I waited for her.

At least that is how I picture our arrival. But as soon as I try to recover the distant memory of that first evening as I waited in the courtyard at Sainte-Agathe, I remember other times when I was waiting for something. Immediately, I see myself, both hands hanging on to the gateway railings, spying anxiously on someone setting off down the main street. If I try to imagine the first night I spent in my attic room above the granary, right away I start remembering other nights. I am no longer alone in the room: a huge, restless, friendly shadow passes along the walls and wanders around. The whole peaceful countryside – the school, old man Martin's field with its three walnut trees, the garden teeming with women at four o'clock each day – is always shaken up and transformed in my mind by the person who turned our adolescence upside down. Even after he disappeared, we were on edge. Yet my family had been at Sainte-Agathe for ten years before Meaulnes arrived.

I was fifteen. It was a cold November Sunday, autumn with the bite of winter. Millie spent the entire day waiting for a carriage from the station to deliver a winter hat. In the morning, she missed Mass, but sent me along anyway, and right up until the sermon, I watched anxiously from the choir stalls hoping to see her enter wearing the new hat.

In the afternoon, I left for vespers, alone again.

'In any case,' she said, trying to console me, while brushing off my clothes with her hand, 'even if the hat had arrived, I would probably have had to spend my Sunday adjusting it.'

We often passed our winter Sundays like this. At the break of dawn, my father set off for some distant, mist-covered pond to fish for pike from a boat. My mother spent all day in her dark room, repairing our humble clothes. She shut herself in like that for fear one of her friends, just as poor and as proud as she, might come and surprise her at it. As for me, after vespers I spent my time reading in the cold dining room, waiting for her to open the door and show me how her efforts had turned out.

That particular Sunday, a ripple of excitement in front of the church kept me behind after vespers. A baptism under the porch had attracted a troop of urchins. In the square, several local men were dressed in their firemen's jackets; lined up, chilled to the bone and stamping their feet, they listened to Boujardon, the drill sergeant, tying himself in theoretical knots.

The carillon for the baptism stopped suddenly as though the bell-ringer realised he had the time and the place wrong. Boujardon and his men, weapons slung over their shoulders, took off with the fire pump at a slow trot. I saw them disappear around the first corner, crushing twigs underfoot with their big boots on the frozen road, followed by four silent lads. I did not have the courage to follow them.

Now the only place in town showing any signs of life was the Café Daniel, from which I could hear the muffled rise and fall of drinkers' arguments. Keeping close to the lower wall of the courtyard separating our house from the village, I arrived back at the little gate, anxious about being late. The gate was open and I immediately perceived something out of the ordinary.

A grey-haired woman was bending over, trying to peep through the curtains of the dining-room door, the closest of the five glass doors which opened on to the courtyard. She was tiny and wore an old-fashioned black velvet bonnet. Her face was narrow and fine-boned but ravaged with anxiety. At this sight, a strange feeling of

7

dread brought me to a halt at the first step in front of the gate.

'Where has he gone? My God!' she muttered. 'He was with me just now. He has already looked around the house. Perhaps he has run off . . .'

Between each phrase, she knocked three times on the pane, so quietly as to be almost inaudible.

Nobody opened the door to the unknown visitor. Millie's hat had clearly been delivered and, seated at the far end of the red room beside a bed strewn with ribbons and feathers, sewing, unpicking, and rebuilding her poorly-made headpiece, she would have been totally unaware of anything else. But when I entered the dining room, closely followed by the visitor, my mother appeared, with both hands to her head, holding together a mass of ribbons, feathers, and gold threads not yet perfectly sewn into place.

She smiled at me, her blue eyes tired from having worked until nightfall, and exclaimed: 'Look! I was waiting to show you . . .'

But seeing the woman seated in the large armchair at the end of the room, she halted, disconcerted. Quickly she removed the hat. During the entire scene that followed, she held it against her breast, upside down like a nest in the crook of her right arm.

The woman in the bonnet kept her umbrella and a leather bag between her knees. She started to explain why she was here, gently nodding her head and tutting like any woman visitor. She had regained her poise, and talked about her son in an intriguing, mysterious, and somewhat superior manner.

They had come in a coach from La Ferté-d'Angillon, fourteen kilometres from Sainte-Agathe. A wealthy widow – or so she would have us believe – she had lost the younger of her children, Antoine. He had died one evening after returning home from school, having stopped to swim with his brother in a dangerously unhealthy pond. She had decided to board her older son, Augustin, with us so that he could study the upper-school curriculum.

Right away she started singing the praises of the scholar she had brought to us. I could no longer recognise the grey-haired woman whom I had seen bent in front of the door a minute before, frantic and pleading like a mother hen about to lose the wildest chick of her brood.

What she told us about her son was startling. He liked to please her and sometimes followed the river's edge for kilometres, bare-legged, to bring her the eggs of moorhens and wild ducks, lost in the furze. He also set up nets, and the other night had found a pheasant caught in a snare in the woods.

I, who dared not come home if I had so much as a little tear in my smock, looked at Millie, astonished.

But my mother was not listening. She even signalled the woman to stop, carefully set her 'nest' down on the table, and rose silently, as if she wanted to take someone by surprise.

Above us, in a small room where blackened fireworks from the previous Fourteenth of July celebrations were heaped up, unfamiliar but confident footsteps paced back and forth, shaking the ceiling. Then they crossed the immense dark loft and faded away towards the assistant masters' empty rooms, which we used now for ripening apples and drying linden blossoms for tea.

'I heard this same noise a little while ago, downstairs,' said Millie softly, 'and I thought it was you, François, coming home.'

No one said anything. We were all standing, hearts beating hard, when the loft door above the kitchen staircase opened. Someone came down the steps, crossed the kitchen, and stood in the dark at the entrance to the dining room.

'Is that you, Augustin?' asked the woman.

All I could see of the tall boy, who seemed to be about seventeen years old, were his peasant's felt hat turned backwards and his black smock pulled in at the waist with a belt the way young schoolboys wear them. I could also just make out that he was smiling. He caught sight of me, and before anyone could demand an explanation, called: 'Come out to the playground!'

I hesitated for a second. Then, as Millie did not restrain me, I grabbed my cap and joined him. We went out through the kitchen door and into the yard where night was rapidly falling. Walking beside him in the faint light, I could just discern his angular face with its straight nose and downy lip.

'Look what I found in your loft,' he said. 'Have you never looked in there?'

He held out a little blackened wheel. A string of rockets, mostly torn to shreds, circled it. It must have been the sun or moon firework from the Fourteenth of July.

'Two didn't go off. We're going to light them now,' he said in a tranquil voice, with the air of someone who hopes that better things lie in store.

He threw his cap on the ground, and I noticed that his head was shaved like a peasant's. He showed me the two rockets whose paper fuses had been touched by flame, blackened, but then abandoned. He stuck the hub of the wheel into the sand, and pulled a box of matches from his pocket – to my great astonishment because for us matches were strictly forbidden. Bending down, he carefully put the flame to the fuse and then grabbing me by the hand, pulled me sharply back.

An instant later, my mother, who had come to the doorstep with his mother after discussing and fixing the price for boarding Augustin, saw two showers of red and white stars shooting up from the playground, hissing. For a brief moment she could see me standing in the magic glow, holding the big newcomer by the hand, not turning a hair.

Again, words deserted her.

That evening at dinner, a stranger ate at our family table, silent, his head lowered, not caring that all three of us were staring fixedly at him.

CHAPTER II

FOUR O'CLOCK IN THE AFTERNOON

UNTIL then, I had hardly ever played with the local boys. A leg injury had left me fearful and unhappy, and I can still see myself chasing after more my more agile schoolmates in the alleys which surrounded the house, hopping along miserably on one leg.

I was hardly ever allowed out. I remember Millie, who was very proud of me, more than once hauling me back to the house and slapping me hard for leaping around on one foot with the village rascals.

The arrival of Augustin Meaulnes, which coincided with my recovery, was the beginning of a new life.

Before he came, after classes finished at four o'clock, I spent the long, lonely evenings by myself. My father carried the burning embers from the classroom stove to the fireplace in the dining room. One by one, the last dawdlers abandoned the increasingly cold, smoky schoolroom. A few final games, some galloping in the playground, then night fell. The two students who had swept the classroom, fetched their caps and capes from the shed and quickly departed, baskets over their arms, leaving the gate wide open.

As long as there was a glimmer of daylight, I repaired to the depths of the town hall and shut myself away in the archives with its dead flies and posters flapping in the draught. I read, seated on an old set of scales, near a window which looked out on to a garden.

When night fell – when the dogs in the neighbouring farm began howling – when our kitchen window lit up – I went home at last. My mother started preparing dinner, and I climbed three steps of the ladder to the loft. I sat down without saying anything, my head resting on the cold rungs above, and watched her start the fire in the narrow kitchen, where a single candle flickered.

But someone had arrived to take away my peaceful childhood pleasures. Someone had blown out the candle which lit up my mother's sweet face as she bent over the evening meal. Someone had extinguished the lamp around which we collected as a happy family at night-time, when my father closed the wooden shutters over the French windows. That person was Augustin Meaulnes, whom the other students soon called Meaulnes the Magnificent.

From the moment he became a boarder at our place at the beginning of December, the school ceased to be deserted after four o'clock in the afternoon. When lessons were over, and in spite of the cold wind that whistled in through the banging door and the cries of the cleaners with their buckets of water, twenty or so senior students, from the country and the town, remained huddled around Meaulnes in the classroom. I hovered around with anxiety and pleasure while they entered into long discussions and interminable disputes.

Meaulnes said nothing, but every so often, to impress him, one of the more talkative students moved into the centre of the group, and using his companions one by one as witnesses, recounted some long story of marauding while they cheered noisily and the rest listened attentively, open-mouthed, laughing silently.

Seated on a desk, swinging his legs, Meaulnes appeared to be lost in thought; however, at the right moments he laughed too, but holding back, as though to reserve his real laughter for some far wittier story, known only to him. Then, as night fell and the light from the classroom windows no longer illuminated the motley crew, he would get up suddenly and burst through the tight circle, shouting: 'Off we go!'

Everyone followed him, and their cries could be heard deep into the night, as far away as the end of town.

By now, I was fit enough to accompany them. I would go with Meaulnes at milking time as far as the entrance to the stables just outside town. Or sometimes we went into a shop where, from the depths, between two creaks of his loom, the weaver would say:

'Here come the students!'

By dinner time we generally found ourselves back near the school, at Desnoues's place. He was a wheelwright and blacksmith, and his smithy was a former inn with huge double doors which he left open. From the street, we could hear the bellows wheezing, and by the light of the blaze in this dark and chiming place, we could sometimes see country people who had stopped their carts to chat for a moment, or sometimes a student like us leaned against a door, looking in but saying nothing.

And that is how, about eight days before Christmas, it all began.

CHAPTER III

AT THE BASKETMAKER'S

THE rain fell all day, only ceasing in the evening. We were bored to death. During break, no one went outside, and in the classroom my father, Monsieur Seurel, cried out time after time, 'Quiet, boys; stop horsing around!'

After the last break, or as we referred to it 'the last quarter of an hour,' Monsieur Seurel, who had been walking pensively to and fro, came to a halt and thwacked his ruler on the table to hush the muddled buzzing that accompanies the restless end of a class. In the expectant silence, he asked:

'Who will accompany François to the station tomorrow to pick up Monsieur and Madame Charpentier?'

These were my grandparents: Grandfather Charpentier was a retired forester who always wore a hooded cloak of grey wool and a rabbit-fur hat, which he called his *kepi*. The boys knew him well. In the mornings he drew a bucket of water to shave with, in the manner of old soldiers, and scraped away vaguely at his goatee. A circle of small children, hands behind their backs, watched him with respectful curiosity. They also knew Grandmother Charpentier, a tiny peasant woman in a knitted bonnet, because at least once Millie had brought her into the junior classroom.

Every year, a few days before Christmas, we went to the station to meet them off the 4.02 train. To visit us, they had to travel across the whole *département*, laden with bags of chestnuts and provisions for Christmas wrapped in napkins. From the moment they stepped over our threshold, still bundled up and smiling, but somewhat stunned by the journey, we shut all the doors behind them, and then began a week of intense pleasure . . .

We needed someone responsible to drive with me to pick them up, someone who would not overturn us in a ditch. But we also needed someone easy-going because Grandfather Charpentier was quick to curse while my grandmother was very garrulous.

A dozen voices responded to Monsieur Seurel's question, yelling out together:

'Meaulnes! Meaulnes. Magnificent Meaulnes!'

But Monsieur Seurel appeared not to hear.

Then some cried:

'Fromentin!'

And others cried:

'Jasmin Delouche!'

The youngest member of the Roy family (known for galloping around the fields, mounted on his sow) screamed out:

'Me! Me!' in a piercing voice.

Dutremblay and Moucheboeuf contented themselves by each raising a timid hand.

I wanted Meaulnes to come with me. That way, the trip in the donkey cart would become an important event. He wanted to come too, but he affected a quiet disdain. All the older students were seated, like him, on the table with their feet on the benches, as we used to in moments of respite or rejoicing. Coffin, his smock pulled up and rolled around his waist, hung on to the iron column which held up the main beam of the classroom and began to shimmy up it gleefully. But Monsieur Seurel cooled everyone down, barking:

'That's enough! It will be Moucheboeuf.'

And we all went back to our places in silence.

At four o'clock, I found myself alone with Meaulnes in the cold courtyard where the rain was making furrows in the sheet of ice that covered the ground. Saying nothing, both of us watched swirls of wind drying off the glistening village. Soon, little Coffin came out of his house, wearing his cap and holding a chunk of bread. Hugging the walls and whistling, he made his way to the blacksmith's. Meaulnes opened the gate, greeted him, and an instant later all three of us had installed ourselves at the glowing, red smithy, feeling warm as toast, in spite of the glacial gusts that blew through the building. Coffin and I sat down next to the forge, our muddy feet in the white wood shavings. Meaulnes leaned against the doorpost with his hands in his pockets, silent. From time to time, a village woman passed by on her way back from the butcher's, her head lowered because of the wind, and we would raise our noses to see who it was.

No one said anything. The blacksmith and his assistant, the one pumping air bellows, the other beating the iron, threw huge, stark shadows on the wall. I remember that particular evening as a high-point of my adolescence. Yet my pleasure was tinged with anxiety. I feared that Meaulnes might spoil my anticipation about driving to the station, but even so, without daring to admit it to myself, I was waiting for him to suggest some extraordinary enterprise which would turn my world upside down.

Every now and then the peaceful regularity of the hammering was interrupted for a moment as, with a ringing clang, the blacksmith let his hammer drop down on the anvil. Picking up, in his leather apron, the piece of iron he was working, he inspected it, and then took a breather to ask, 'So, lads, how are things going?'

His assistant kept one hand in the air on the bellows chain, put his left fist on his hip, and looked at us with a laugh.

Then the heavy, deafening work resumed.

During one of these pauses, we caught sight of Millie through the door, laden with parcels, her head bound up in a scarf, battling against the strong wind. The blacksmith asked us:

'Is Monsieur Charpentier coming soon?'

'Tomorrow,' I replied, 'with my grandmother. I am going to fetch them off the 4.02 train.'

'In Fromentin's carriage?'

'No, in old man Martin's cart,' I quickly replied.

'Oh, then you'll be gone for ever!'

The blacksmith and his assistant both began to laugh, and then for the sake of saying something, anything, the assistant drawled:

'With Fromentin's mare you could pick them up at Vierzon. The train waits there for an hour. It's fifteen kilometres away, and you could get back before Martin's donkey was even hitched up.'

'She's a fast horse!' the other said.

'And I know for sure that Fromentin would gladly lend her.'

The conversation ended there. Once more the shop became a place of sparks and clanging, with each of us thinking his own thoughts.

When the time came to leave and I got up to signal Meaulnes, he did not notice me at first. Leaning against the door with his head bent, he seemed profoundly absorbed by what had just been said. Seeing him like that, lost in reflection, looking as though he were peering across a foggy landscape at those peaceful workmen, I was suddenly reminded of the image recalled by Robinson Crusoe of himself as a young boy who used to be often found at a basket-maker's shop, years before his momentous departure.

I have often thought about it since.

CHAPTER IV

THE ESCAPE

AT one o'clock in the afternoon of the following day, the senior classroom is a bright spot in the middle of the icy countryside, like a little boat in the middle of the ocean, except that one can smell neither the dirty grease nor the brine of a fishing vessel, but rather herrings grilled on the stove and scorched wool from those who are warming themselves too close to the heat.

Because it is nearing the end of the year, test books have been distributed to us. While Monsieur Seurel writes questions on the blackboard, an uneasy silence settles in, interrupted by soft-voiced conversations, stifled little cries, and short phrases with which to frighten one's neighbour:

'Monsieur! He . . .'

Monsieur Seurel thinks about other matters as he copies out the questions. He turns around from time to time, giving us a look that is both absent and severe. At once, the surreptitious commotion ceases entirely, for a moment, only to begin again, softly at first, like purring.

I alone remain silent in the middle of this agitation. Seated near the big windows at the end of one of the tables with the youngest group, I have only to stretch upwards a little in order to see the garden, the stream at the end of the garden, and then the fields.

From time to time, I rise up on tiptoe and look anxiously towards Belle-Etoile farm. Since class began, I have been aware that Meaulnes has not come back after the midday break. The boy who sits next to him must also have perceived this, but he has said nothing yet, preoccupied by his test. However, as soon as he lifts his head, the news will rip through the whole class, and someone will yell out:

'Monsieur! Meaulnes . . .'

I know that Meaulnes has gone. More precisely, I have a hunch that he has made a run for it. As soon as we finished lunch, he must have jumped over the little wall, slipped across the fields, crossed the stream at Vieille-Planche, and arrived at Belle-Etoile. Once there, he would have asked to borrow the mare in order to fetch Monsieur and Madame Charpentier from the station. He would be hitching her up right now.

The farm at Belle-Etoile stands on a hillside slope across the stream, on a track which joins up with the road to the station at one end and with a straggling hamlet at the other. In summer, the large farmyard is hidden by elms and oaks and hedges. The grand, feudal building, surrounded by high walls and underpinned by buttresses wallowing in manure, cannot be seen for leaves in June. At nightfall all one can hear is the rolling of carts and the cries of cowherds. But today, through my window, I can see, through the leafless trees, the high grey wall of the farmyard, and its entrance. Beyond, I can make out between the sections of fence, a strip of frost-whitened track, parallel to the stream, leading to the station road.

Nothing moves in this clear winter landscape. Nothing has changed – yet.

Here in the classroom, Monsieur Seurel finishes copying the second question on the blackboard. He usually gives us three. Perhaps he will only give us two today . . . He will go back to his chair and then notice Meaulnes's absence. He will send two boys to look for him all over town and they will certainly manage to find him before the mare is hitched up.

Instead, having copied the second question, Monsieur Seurel lets his tired arm drop for an instant, then to my great relief goes back to the board and starts writing again, saying:

'Now, this one is child's play!'

I notice what look like two little black stakes, which must be the shafts of a cart, pass by the Belle-Etoile wall and disappear. I am sure now that someone over there is making preparations for Meaulnes's departure. Now here is the mare, her head and forequarters passing between the two pillars of the entrance. Now she stops while someone fixes a second bench into the back of the cart for the passengers that Meaulnes claims to be picking up from the station. At last, between two gaps in the hedge, I see the carriage slowly leaving the courtyard, disappearing for an instant behind the hedge, and passing again at the same slow pace on to the white road. Then I recognise the black shape holding the reins, elbow resting nonchalantly like a peasant's on the side of the cart; it is my friend, Augustin Meaulnes.

A moment later, everything disappears behind the hedge. Two men standing at the gate to Belle-Etoile, watching the cart's departure, consult each other with growing animation. One of them at last decides to put his hands to his mouth like a megaphone. He shouts out to Meaulnes, then runs several steps after him along the track. But then, as soon as the cart makes it on to the station road and is no longer visible from the path, Meaulnes suddenly changes his posture. He stands up, with one foot in front like a Roman charioteer, and slaps the reins, urging the mare forward at full speed. In an instant he disappears over the rise. On the track, the man who had been yelling at him begins to run again; the other man hurls himself across the fields. He is coming our way.

A few minutes later, at the moment when Monsieur Seurel leaves the blackboard and rubs his hands together to get rid of the chalk, at the very moment when three voices cry out as one from the back of the classroom, 'Sir! Meaulnes has gone!' the farmer in his blue smock is at the door. He flings it open, raises his hat, and asks from the threshold:

'Excuse me, sir, did you authorise a student to order a coach to go to Vierzon to pick up your parents? Things seem a bit suspicious.'

'Certainly not!' replies Monsieur Seurel.

Immediately the class is in an appalling uproar. The three students nearest the door rush outside. They are the ones usually in charge of stoning the goats and pigs who come into the courtyard to snuffle around among the treasures of the dustbins. The violent sound of their hobnailed clogs on the flagstones is succeeded by the muffled crunch of their rapid steps on the sand in the playground and their skidding at the bend where the iron gate opens on to the street. The rest of the class piles up at the windows that overlook the garden. Some even climb on the tables to see better.

But it is too late. Meaulnes has vanished.

'All the same, you will go to the station with Moucheboeuf,' Monsieur Seurel informs me. 'Meaulnes does not know the Vierzon road. He will get confused at the crossroads, and it will take him at least three hours to get to the train.'

Millie sticks her head through the doorway of the lower class-room and demands: 'What is going on?'

People begin to gather in the main street. The farmer is still obstinately standing there, hat in hand, like someone demanding justice.

CHAPTER V

THE CARRIAGE RETURNS

AFTER I had picked them up from the station and they were seated in front of the big fireplace after dinner, my grandparents began to recount in minute detail all that had happened since the last holidays. I soon realised I was not listening.

The courtyard's iron gate was near the dining-room door, and it always squeaked when it was opened. Usually, during those interminable, country evenings, I waited, secretly hoping the gate would squeak, to be followed by the sound of clogs clattering or being wiped on the step, and the whisper of people conferring before entering. Then someone would knock: a neighbour, some teachers, anyone who might arrive at last to divert us.

That particular evening, I needed nothing from outside since all those I loved were together in our house. Even so, I did not stop listening to the night sounds, expecting someone to open our door.

My old grandfather, bushy-faced as an old Gascon shepherd, sat with both feet planted heavily in front of him, his walking stick between his knees, and leaned forward to knock his pipe against his shoe. With his kind, watery eyes he confirmed what my grandmother was saying about the journey and her hens and her neighbours and the tenants who had not yet paid their rent. But I was no longer paying attention.

I was imagining the rolling of a carriage and its sudden stop in front of our door. Meaulnes would jump out and saunter in as though nothing had happened. Or perhaps he would first lead the mare back to Belle-Etoile; and I would soon hear the sound of his steps on the road and the gate opening.

But nothing happened. My grandfather gazed steadfastly ahead and when his eyelids blinked they stayed closed longer and longer as sleep overtook him. Embarrassed, my grandmother had to repeat what she had just said, but still no one listened.

'Are you upset about this boy?' she asked at last.

I had questioned her in vain at the station. She had seen no one who resembled Meaulnes at Vierzon. He must have been delayed en route, and his daring exploit gone awry. During our return in the coach, I mulled over my disappointment while my grandmother chatted with Moucheboeuf. Along the frost-covered road, little birds whirled away from the donkey's feet as he trotted. The distant call of a shepherdess or of a boy hailing his companion from one thicket of fir trees to another rose from time to time above the quiet of the frozen afternoon. Each time, this cry from the desolate hills made me tremble as if it were Meaulnes's voice inviting me to follow him into the distance . . .

Bedtime arrived while I was mulling this over. My grandfather had already left for the red room, the bedroom-cum-sitting room, damp and freezing from being shut since the previous winter. My mother had removed the lace antimacassars from the armchairs, taken up the rugs, and placed fragile objects to one side so that he could install himself comfortably. He had laid his stick on a straight chair, his big shoes on an armchair, and had just blown out his candle. The rest of us were standing up, saying good night to one another, ready to go our separate ways for the night, when the sound of wheels silenced us.

It sounded like two vehicles, one following the other at a very slow trot. They slowed down further and finally came to a stop outside the dining-room window, which had once looked on to the road, but was sealed up now.

My father picked up the lamp and quickly opened the door he had just locked. Then, pushing the gate open, he stood at the top of the steps and lifted the light high above his head so he could see what was going on.

Two carriages had indeed stopped, the horse of one attached behind the other carriage. A man jumped to the ground and hesitated.

'Is this the village hall?' he asked as he approached. 'Where can I find Monsieur Fromentin, the tenant farmer at Belle-Etoile? I've found his carriage and his mare without a driver going along the Saint-Loup-des-Bois road. With my lantern, I was able to make out his name and address on the plate. I have brought back the carriage as I was going this way, but it has made me very late.'

We stood there stupefied. My father went closer and shone his lamp on the carriage.

'There was no trace at all of a traveller,' continued the man. 'Not even a blanket. The beast is tired; she is limping a little.'

I moved forward and looked with the others at this lost horse and carriage that had come back to us, like a wreck thrown up by a high sea – the first wreck, but perhaps not the last, of Meaulnes's adventure.

'If Fromentin lives too far away,' said the man, 'I will leave the carriage with you. I've already lost a lot of time and they'll be worried about me at home.'

My father agreed. In this way, we would be able to take the horse and carriage back to Belle-Etoile straight away, without explaining what had happened. Then we could decide what to tell the locals and what to write to Meaulnes's mother. We offered the man a glass of wine, but he cracked his whip and galloped away.

My father drove off in the carriage, while we went silently back into the house. My grandfather had relit his candle and was shouting from the depths of his room:

'So! Has the traveller returned?'

The women looked at each other for a moment.

'Yes, he was at his mother's. Go to sleep, and don't worry any more.'

'Good. So much the better. It's exactly what I thought,' he said. Satisfied, he blew out his candle and rolled over to sleep.

This was the same explanation we gave to the villagers. As for the fugitive's mother, we decided to wait before writing to her, and we kept our anxiety to ourselves for three long days. I can still remember my father's return from Belle-Etoile towards eleven o'clock, his moustache damp from the night air, and his talking to Millie in a low, anguished, angry voice.

CHAPTER VI

A KNOCK AT THE WINDOW

THE fourth day was one of the coldest that winter. Early in the morning, the first arrivals slid on the ice around the well to keep themselves warm. They were waiting until the stove was lit inside the school and they could hurl themselves in its direction.

Several of us lay in wait just inside the gate for the boys from the countryside. They arrived dazzled by the frosty landscape they had just traversed, having gazed at frozen ponds and copses into which the hares had bolted. Their smocks reeked of hay and the stable, and when they pressed around the glowing stove, the classroom air became redolent with the smell. That particular morning, one of them had found a frozen squirrel on the road and had brought it along in a basket. I remember he tried to attach the long stiff beast by its claws to an upright supporting the playground roof.

Then the tedious winter lessons began.

A sudden knock on the window pane made us lift our heads. We saw Meaulnes standing at the door, brushing the frost off his shirt, his head high, his eyes dazed.

The two students on the bench nearest the door sprang up to open it. There was a muted discussion at the entry, which we did not hear, and at last the fugitive decided to come inside the school.

A gust of fresh air from the deserted playground, stalks of hay attached Meaulnes's clothes, above all his air of a traveller, exhausted and starving, but overcome by wonder – all this made us shiver with pleasure and curiosity.

Monsieur Seurel, who was giving us dictation, took two steps down from his desk, and Meaulnes marched towards him aggressively. I remember how noble my tall friend looked at that moment, in spite of his exhaustion and his red eyes, red no doubt from spending the nights outside.

He advanced towards the rostrum and said in the assured voice of someone who is bringing back information:

'I have returned, sir.'

'So I see,' replied Monsieur Seurel, looking at him with curiosity. 'Sit down at your desk.'

Meaulnes turned towards us, his back a little bent, smiling a mocking smile the way the older undisciplined students did when they were punished. Seizing the end of the table with one hand, he slid himself on to the bench.

'You will read a book I recommend,' said the teacher – all heads were turned towards Meaulnes – 'while your classmates finish their dictation.'

The lesson resumed. From time to time, Meaulnes turned towards me, and then looked out of the windows. Through them we could see the white garden, white as cotton and still, and beyond the garden deserted fields where a crow occasionally landed. In the classroom, the heat was oppressive near the red-hot stove. My friend, head in hands, leaned on his elbows to read; twice I saw his eyelids close and I thought he was going to sleep.

'I would like to go to bed, sir,' he said at last, raising his hand half-way. 'I haven't slept for three nights.'

'Go!' said Monsieur Seurel, wishing above all to avoid an incident.

With heads raised, pens poised in the air, we all watched with regret as he left, the back of his smock crumpled, his shoes caked in mud.

How slowly the morning crept along! As noon approached, we heard the traveller preparing to descend from the attic above. At lunch I found him seated in front of the fire, near my dumbfounded grandparents. Just at that moment, the clock struck twelve, and the seniors and juniors, who were scattered around the snowy schoolyard, gathered in front of the door to the dining room like a line of shadows.

I remember nothing about this meal but gaping silence and embarrassment. Everything was frigid: the bare oilcloth, the cold wine in the glasses, the red tiles on which we placed our feet. We had decided not to question the fugitive in case we turned him against us. He took advantage of this respite and said nothing.

At last, pudding finished, we could dash out into the yard; an afternoon schoolyard where clogs had turned the snow to slush, a schoolyard where snowmelt dripped from the roofs, a schoolyard filled with games and piercing shrieks! Meaulnes and I stayed close to the buildings as we ran along. Two or three of our friends from the town left the main group and ran towards us, yelling with joy, squishing mud under their clogs, their hands in their pockets, their scarves flying. But my companion hurled himself into the senior schoolroom, and I shot in after him and shut the door just in time to withstand the assault of those who were following us. Then came a thunderous, violent sound of shaken windowpanes, of clogs hammering on the threshold, and a shove which bent the iron rod supporting the two halves of the door. But Meaulnes, at the risk of cutting himself on its jagged ring, had already turned the key in the lock.

We always found this kind of incursion very irritating. During the summer, boys left outside the door like this would gallop around the garden and often managed to climb in through the windows before we had a chance to shut them all. But now it was December and everything was closed. One moment they were throwing their weight against the door and hurling insults at us; the next moment they turned their backs and left, one by one, heads down, adjusting their scarves.

In the classroom, which smelled of chestnuts and cheap wine, two cleaners were moving the tables around. I went over to the stove and warmed myself idly while waiting for classes to resume. Meanwhile, Meaulnes was searching the teacher's bureau and the students' desks. He soon came across an atlas which he began to study passionately, standing on the rostrum, his elbows on the desk, his head in his hands.

I prepared to join him. I would have put my hand on his shoulder and we would have without doubt traced together on the map the journey he had made, but suddenly Jasmin Delouche flung open the door from the junior classroom. He was followed by a boy from the town and three others from the country, who all surged in with a triumphant cry. One of the windows of the junior classroom must not have been properly closed; they had pushed it open and jumped in.

Though still on the short side, Jasmin Delouche was one of the oldest boys in the senior school. He was extremely jealous of Meaulnes, even though he pretended to be his friend. Before the arrival of our boarder, Jasmin was cock of the walk. He had a pale, rather bland, face and greased-down hair. The only son of the widow Delouche, an innkeeper, he pretended to be a man, always proudly repeating what he overheard the billiard players and vermouth drinkers saying in the bar.

On his entrance, Meaulnes raised his head and, frowning, shouted at the boys who were jostling to get close to the stove:

'Can't one have a moment's peace around here?'

'If you're not happy with it, you should have stayed where you were,' replied Jasmin Delouche, without raising his head, his confidence boosted by the support of his friends.

I think Augustin was in that state of utter fatigue where anger mounts up and takes you by surprise so there is nothing you can do about it.

'You,' he said, pale-faced, standing up and shutting his book, 'get out of here.'

The other sniggered and shouted:

'Oh ho! Because you escaped from here for three days, you think you're the boss now?' And bringing his associates into the quarrel, he said: 'You can't make us leave, you know!'

Meaulnes was already on him. They tore into each other, ripping shirtsleeves and seams. Only Martin, one of the country boys who had entered with Jasmin, dared to intervene.

'Let him go!' he said, his nostrils flaring, shaking his head like a ram.

With one violent shove, Meaulnes threw him, tottering with arms outstretched, into the middle of the classroom. Then, with one hand he grabbed Delouche by the neck and with the other opened the door and tried to throw him outside. Jasmin clutched at the tables and dragged his feet on the tiles, his hobnailed boots screeching, while Martin, who had regained his balance, marched back, his head thrust forward, full of rage. Meaulnes let go of Delouche to grab this imbecile. He could have found himself in a tight spot, but just then the door to our room opened halfway, and Monsieur Seurel appeared, head turned towards the kitchen, finishing a conversation with someone before entering.

The fight stopped immediately. Those boys who had narrowly avoided taking part gathered around the stove, their heads bowed. Meaulnes sat down in his place, the tops of his sleeves ripped and torn at the seams. As for Jasmin, he was red in the face and could be heard shouting during the few seconds that preceded the rap of the ruler that signalled the beginning of class:

'He can't go on like this. He thinks he's so clever. Perhaps he thinks we don't know where he's been.'

'Idiot. I don't even know myself,' said Meaulnes in the already gaping silence.

Then he hunched his shoulders, placed his head in his hands, and settled down to his studies.

CHAPTER VII

THE SILK WAISTCOAT

OUR bedroom was in a large loft. Half attic, half bedroom. The assistant masters' rooms had windows; no one knew why this one had a skylight instead. The door scraped along the floor, and it was impossible to shut it completely. When we went upstairs at night, sheltering our candles from draughts with a hand, we tried to shut the door each time, and each time we had to give up. And all night the silence of the three lofts surrounded us, and encroached on our room.

Augustin and I met up again in our room on the evening of that same winter's day.

I flung off my clothes quickly and threw them in a heap on a chair at the head of my bed, but my companion undressed slowly, saying nothing. Once ensconced in my iron bed, I watched him from behind its vine-decorated curtains. At times he sat down on his low, curtainless bed; then he got up and walked to and fro as he undressed. He placed his candle on a little wicker table (which had been woven by gypsies) and the light threw his huge, wandering shadow across the wall.

Unlike me, he folded and arranged his school uniform with care, but with a bitter and distracted look. I watched as he laid his heavy belt on a chair, folded his extraordinarily crumpled, dirty smock on the back of it, pulled off a dark blue jacket he wore under his smock, and, with his back to me, bent to spread it at the foot of his bed. When he stood up and turned towards me, I saw he was wearing, instead of the little waistcoat with brass buttons that went

31

with his school jacket, a strange silk waistcoat, open at the top but fastened at the bottom with a serried row of mother-of-pearl buttons.

It was a garment from a charming fantasy, something young men who danced with our grandmothers wore to balls in the 1830s.

I can still recall that big, country schoolboy – bare-headed now because he had carefully placed his cap on top of his other clothes – his young face so valiant but so hardened already. He began pacing the room again, unbuttoning the mysterious garment which clearly came from a costume that did not belong to him. It was strange to see him in his shirtsleeves, too-short trousers, and muddy shoes handling the waistcoat of a marquis.

Touching it, he came out of his reverie and looked at me with troubled eyes. I felt a bit like laughing. He smiled at the same time as I did and his face cleared. This gave me courage to speak.

'Oh! Tell me what it is,' I said softly. 'Where did you get it?'

Immediately his smile disappeared. He ran a heavy hand twice over his close-cropped hair and suddenly, like someone who could no longer resist the urge, pulled his jacket back on and firmly buttoned it over the fine frills, and then covered everything with his crumpled smock. He hesitated for a moment, glancing sideways at me. Finally, he sat on the edge of his bed and let his shoes fall noisily to the floor. Fully dressed, like a soldier at the ready, he stretched out on his bed and blew out the candle.

Around midnight, I awoke suddenly. Meaulnes was standing in the middle of the room, his cap on his head, looking for something on the coatstand – a cape he then put on his back. The room was very dark, without even reflected light from the snow. A black and icy wind blew through the dead garden and over the roof.

I raised myself up a bit, and called softly to him.

'Meaulnes! Are you leaving again?'

He did not reply. Panic-stricken, I said:

'All right then, I'm leaving with you. You have to take me along.' And I jumped out of bed.

He came towards me, grabbed me by the arm, and forced me to sit down, saying:

'I cannot take you, François. If I knew the way, you could certainly accompany me. But I must find it on the map, and I haven't managed that yet.'

'Then you can't leave either!'

'That's right. It's useless,' he said, discouraged. 'Go on, go back to bed. I promise not to leave without you.'

He began pacing up and down the room again. I no longer dared speak. He walked, stopped, and then started up again more quickly, like someone who, in his head, seeks out and relives memories, confronts them, compares them, calculates, and suddenly finds something; then loses the thread and begins searching again.

This was not the only night when, wakened by the sound of his footsteps towards one o'clock in the morning, I found him wandering around in our bedroom and the lofts — like one of those sailors who cannot break the habit of keeping watch and who, back in the depths of the Breton countryside, rises and dresses at the required hour to keep vigil over the rural night.

Two or three times during the month of January and the first two weeks of February, I was wakened in this way. Meaulnes would be there, standing up, kitted out with his cape on his back, ready to leave. But each time, just as he seemed on the verge of setting off for the mysterious domain to which he had previously escaped, he stopped and hesitated, holding back at the moment of lifting the latch of the door to the stairway and stealing past the kitchen door, which he could easily open without anyone hearing. Instead, during the long midnight hours, he walked feverishly up and down the abandoned lofts, thinking.

At last, one night towards the 15th February, he woke me up himself, placing his hand gently on my shoulder.

The day had been hectic. Meaulnes, who had completely given

up playing with his old friends, had stayed seated at his bench during the last break of the afternoon, totally absorbed in drawing up a secret map and calculating distances with his finger on the atlas of the Cher region. Meanwhile, an incessant to-and-fro took place between the schoolyard and the classroom. Clogs clacked. Boys chased each other from table to table, leaping over benches and even vaulting over the rostrum with one stride. We knew it would be unwise to go near Meaulnes while he was working so hard, but as break wore on, two or three boys from the village approached him playfully, stalking him like wolves, and peered over his shoulder. One of them even dared to shove the others against Meaulnes. He snapped the atlas shut, concealed the paper, and grabbed the nearest of the three boys while the other two managed to escape.

He had caught the spiteful Giraudat, who tried whining and kicking, and when Meaulnes chucked him outside at the end of the tussle, shrieked back at him furiously:

'You big coward! It doesn't surprise me that everyone is against you, that everyone wants to fight you!' He yelled a heap of other insults to which we replied without properly understanding what he was saying. I shouted the loudest because I was on Meaulnes's side. We now had an understanding. The promise he had given to take me with him, without saying like the rest that I 'couldn't walk straight', had bound me to him for ever. I couldn't stop thinking about the mysterious journey. I had persuaded myself that he had met a young woman. She was without doubt infinitely more beautiful than all the local girls: more beautiful than Jeanne, whom we admired in the nuns' garden (through a keyhole); than Madelaine, the baker's daughter, all pink and blonde; than Jenny, who lived in a castle and was wonderful but mad and always shut away. He was certainly thinking about a young woman every night, like the hero in a novel. I had decided to tackle him about this the next time he woke me up.

On the evening of this latest fight, we were both occupied putting away garden tools, picks and shovels that had been used for digging holes, when we heard cries coming from the road. It was a gang of youths, marching in step, four by four in a column, moving like a perfectly organised squad, and led by Delouche, Daniel, Giraudat, and another whom we didn't know. They saw us and started jeering. It seemed as though the whole town was against us, and they were preparing some kind of war game from which we were excluded.

Without saying a word, Meaulnes returned the spade and pick he was carrying on his shoulder to the shed.

At midnight, I felt his hand on my arm and woke with a start.

'Get up,' he said. 'We're leaving.'

'Do you know the way now, as far as the end?'

'I know a good part of it. And we must seek out the rest!' he replied through clenched teeth.

'Listen, Meaulnes,' I said, sitting up. 'Listen to me: there's only one thing to do, and that is for both of us to look for the missing section during the day, using your map.'

'But that section is far from here.'

'Well, we'll go in a cart this summer, as soon as the days are longer.'

A long silence implied that he had accepted my suggestion.

'Then together we will try to find the young woman you love, Meaulnes,' I added at last. 'Tell me who she is. Tell me all about her.'

He sat down at the foot of my bed. In spite of the darkness, I could just discern his bent head, his crossed arms, his knees. Then he breathed deeply, like someone who has long endured a heavy heart and who was at last going to divulge his secret.

CHAPTER VIII

THE ADVENTURE

THAT night my friend did not explain everything that happened to him on the road. And even later, when he decided to tell me the whole story, during those distressing days which I will talk about again, it remained the great secret of our adolescence. Today, now that everything is finished and nothing but dust remains

of so much evil, of so much good

I can describe his strange adventure.

At half past one in the afternoon, en route to Vierzon in freezing weather, Meaulnes made the mare jog along at a clip because he did not have much time. At first, to amuse himself, he thought about how astonished we would all be when he brought Monsieur and Madame Charpentier back by four o'clock. Certainly, at that moment, he had no other intention.

Little by little the cold penetrated him, and he wrapped his legs in the blanket he had tried at first to refuse, but which the people at Belle-Etoile had forcibly planted in the carriage.

At two o'clock he drove through the village of La Motte. He had never spent time in such a little place during school hours, and he was amused to see it so deserted, so sleepy. Occasionally, here and there, a curtain parted, revealing the head of a curious housewife.

At the far end of La Motte, soon after its schoolhouse, he hesitated between two roads and thought he remembered he should turn left for Vierzon. No one was around to give directions. He started the mare trotting along the road, which became increasingly narrow and stony. He travelled alongside a wood of fir trees for a while and came across a man driving a cart. Using his hand like a megaphone, he asked the man if he was definitely on the road to Vierzon. The mare pulled on the reins and continued to trot, and the man must not have understood what he was being asked. He called out something, made a vague gesture, and Meaulnes randomly continued along the same road.

Once again he was faced with the vast frozen countryside and nothing to break it up or distract him other than an occasional magpie, frightened by the cart, flying up and perching on a dead elm. Meaulnes wrapped the big blanket around his shoulders like a cape. With his legs stretched out and his elbow resting on the side of the cart, he must have dozed off for quite a long time.

When he came to, thanks to the cold which cut through the blanket, the scenery had changed. It was no longer one of distant horizons and a great white sky as far as the eye could see, but instead it was one of meadows, still green, and high hedges. At left and right, water from the ditches ran beneath the ice. Everything spoke of the nearness of a river. And between the hedges, the track was nothing more than a narrow, rutted path.

The mare had stopped trotting. With a crack of his whip, Meaulnes encouraged her to pick up her pace, but she persisted in walking extremely slowly. The tall lad rested his hands on the front of the carriage, looked down one side, and recognised straight away that she was lame in one of her hind legs. He jumped to the ground immediately, very concerned.

'We'll never get to Vierzon in time for the train,' he muttered.

He did not dare confess his most disturbing thought – that perhaps he had made a mistake and was not on the road to Vierzon.

He spent a long time examining the mare's hoof and discovered no trace of a wound. She lifted her foot fearfully whenever Meaulnes tried to feel it and pawed the ground with the heavy, awkward shoe. He realised at last that she had a pebble stuck in the shoe. Expert in the handling of animals, he crouched down and tried to take the right hoof with his left hand and to set it between his knees, but the cart was in the way. Twice the mare took off and advanced several metres, causing the carriage step to hit him on the head and the wheel to injure his knee. He persisted and finally triumphed over the frightened beast; but the pebble was so deeply embedded that Meaulnes had to resort to his peasant's knife to flick it out.

When he had finished the task and lifted his head, dazed and bleary-eyed, he noticed with a shock that night was falling . . .

Anyone other than Meaulnes would have retraced his steps immediately. It was the only way to avoid becoming even more lost. But he thought he must be very far from La Motte by now; and besides, the mare could have followed a crossroad while he slept; and finally, this path must eventually lead towards some village or other. Add to all these reasons that Meaulnes, as he climbed back on to the running board while the impatient beast pulled at the reins, felt a mounting and exasperating desire to achieve *something,* and to arrive *somewhere,* in spite of all the obstacles!

He whipped the mare, who shied and set off at a lively trot. The darkness deepened. The rutted path was just wide enough for the cart. Occasionally a dead branch from the hedge would catch in the wheel and snap with a dry crack . . . When it was completely dark, Meaulnes suddenly thought, with a tightening in his chest, of the dining room at Sainte-Agathe, where we would all be gathered by now. Then anger took hold of him; then pride and a profound joy at having escaped – without even wanting to . . .

CHAPTER IX

STOPPED SHORT

SUDDENLY the mare slackened her pace, as though her hoof had bumped against something in the shadows. Meaulnes saw her head plunge and lift again twice; then she stopped dead, nostrils to the ground, apparently smelling something. He heard water lapping around her feet. A stream cut across the path. In summer this must have been a ford, but at this time of year the current was so strong that ice had not formed, and it was dangerous to push ahead.

Meaulnes pulled gently on the reins to move the mare back several paces and stood up in the cart, perplexed. Then he glimpsed a light through the branches. Only two or three fields must have separated him from the path.

He dismounted and pulled the mare further back, speaking to her soothingly to stop her tossing her head in fear.

'Come on, old girl! Come on! We're not going much further. We'll soon know where we are.'

Pushing open the gate to a small meadow, he ushered the horse and carriage through. His feet sank in the wet grass. The carriage jolted along silently. With his head against the mare's, he could feel her warmth and her heavy breathing. He led her to the end of the meadow, and put the blanket over her back; then parting the branches in the hedge, he saw the light again, coming from an isolated house.

He still had to cross another three meadows and jump over a treacherous stream, which meant plunging both feet in at the same time. At last, after a final leap from the top of an embankment, he found himself in the courtyard of a simple country house. A pig grunted in its sty. At the sound of feet on the icy path, a dog began barking furiously.

The front shutters were open, and the light Meaulnes had seen came from logs in the fireplace. There was no light other than the fire. Inside the house, a woman got up and came to the door without seeming particularly startled. Just at that moment, a grandfather clock struck half past seven.

'Forgive me, my dear lady,' said the tall youth, 'I'm afraid I have trodden on your chrysanthemums.'

She stopped short, bowl in hand, and stared at him.

'Yes,' she said. 'It's so dark in the courtyard that it's impossible to find your way.'

A silence followed, while Meaulnes studied the walls of the room, which were covered with illustrated newspapers like those of an inn, and the table on which a man's hat was resting.

'The master of the house is out?' he asked, sitting down.

'He'll be back in no time,' replied his wife, confidently. 'He's just gone to fetch another log.'

'It's not that I need him,' continued the young man, pulling his chair up to the fire. 'But several of us hunters are out there, looking for game. I've come to ask if you can spare us a bit of bread.'

Meaulnes knew that with country people, especially those in an isolated farm, it was necessary to speak discreetly, diplomatically, and above all never to show that one was a stranger.

'Bread?' she said. 'We can hardly spare you any. The baker who comes by every Tuesday didn't show up today.'

Augustin, who had been hoping to find himself near a village, was alarmed.

'Which baker?' he asked.

'The baker from Vieux-Nançay, of course,' she replied, astonished that he didn't know.

'How far exactly is Vieux-Nançay from here?' continued Meaulnes anxiously.

'By road I wouldn't know how to tell you precisely; but if you take the short cut it would be three and a half leagues.'

She began recounting how her daughter lived there and came on foot to visit her every first Sunday of the month, and that her employers . . . and so on.

Totally disconcerted, Meaulnes interrupted:

'Is Vieux-Nançay the closest village to here?'

'No. That's Les Landes, five kilometres away. But there are no merchants there, not even a baker, just a little public gathering once a year on St Martin's day.'

Meaulnes had never heard of Les Landes. By this time he felt so lost that he was almost amused. But the woman, busy washing her bowl in the sink, turned back to him, curious now, and asked slowly, looking him straight in the eye:

'You're not from round here?'

At that moment, an elderly peasant came through the door with an armful of wood which he threw on the tiled floor. The woman explained to him very loudly, as though he were deaf, what the young man wanted.

'Well, that's easy,' he said simply. 'But come closer to the fire, sir. You're not getting warm enough.'

A moment later both of them had settled down next to the fire, the old man snapping twigs to add to the flames, while Meaulnes feasted on the bowl of bread and milk he had been given. Overjoyed to find himself in this humble house after so many vicissitudes, he thought that his strange adventure was over, and was already planning to return with some companions to visit these good people. He did not realise this was merely a brief rest, and that he would shortly be on the road again.

Meaulnes asked his hosts to show him the road to La Motte. Gradually coming closer to the truth, he explained how he and his carriage had become separated from the other hunters, and he was now completely lost.

The couple kept insisting that he spend the night and not leave until daylight. Meaulnes finally accepted their offer, and went outside to collect the mare and bring her back to the stable.

'Watch out for the ruts in the path,' advised the man.

Meaulnes did not dare admit that he had not used the path, and was just about to ask the kind man to accompany him and show him the way. He hesitated for a second on the threshold, wavering. Then he walked out into the dark farmyard.

CHAPTER X

THE SHEEPFOLD

TO find his bearings, he climbed up the embankment from which he had previously jumped.

Slowly and with difficulty, he guided himself through grass and water and over the willow hedges, as he had done before, and set about finding the carriage where he had left it at the end of the meadow. But it was no longer there. He stood stock still, his head throbbing, and forced himself to listen to the night sounds, believing at each second that he heard the jangle of the mare's collar. Nothing. He circled the meadow; the gate was half open, half knocked over, as if the wheel of a carriage had passed over it. The mare must have escaped this way by herself.

Going back up the track, he took a few paces before he tripped over the blanket. It must have slipped off the mare's back, and he concluded that she had gone in this same direction. He began to run.

With nothing in mind, other than an obstinate and crazed determination to find his carriage, he tore along, red in the face and panic-stricken. From time to time his foot caught in a rut. At bends in the road, he careered into hedges, and too tired to stop before the turn, with his arms out to protect his face, he crashed into the thorns, which tore his hands. Sometimes he stopped, listened, and set off again. At one point he believed he heard the sound of a carriage; but it was nothing but a jolting rubbish cart, passing by far away on a road to his left.

His knee, injured earlier on the carriage step, began to hurt badly and he had to stop because his leg was getting stiff. He reflected that the mare must have galloped away; otherwise he would have caught up with her long before. He also told himself that no carriage could disappear into thin air; someone must have found it. Finally, he turned back on his tracks, exhausted, angry, barely dragging himself along.

At length, he reckoned he had arrived back in the area he had left earlier, and soon he saw the house light he was looking for. A deep path opened up beyond the hedge.

'Here's the route the old man told me about,' Augustin said to himself.

He started down the path, happy that he no longer had to climb over hedges and embankments. A moment later, when the path deviated to the left, the light appeared to slide to the right. Coming to a crossroads, Meaulnes in his hurry to get back to the little dwelling, and without thinking twice, followed the path which seemed to lead directly there. Scarcely had he taken ten steps in this direction when the light disappeared, either because it was hidden by a hedge, or because the couple, tired of waiting, had closed their shutters. Without thinking, he darted across the fields, and made straight for the direction where the light had burned before. Then, having climbed over yet another hedge, he came upon a new path.

Thus, little by little, Meaulnes's route became muddled and he lost his way back to the old couple's house.

Discouraged, with barely any strength left, he resolved in his despair to follow this path to its end. A hundred steps on, he came out into a large, grey meadow with shadows of what must have been juniper bushes here and there, and the darker shadow of a building in a fold in the landscape. Meaulnes approached it. It was a sort of animal pen or abandoned sheepfold. The door gave way with a groan. When the strong wind chased away the clouds, the moonlight shone through cracks in the partitions. A strong smell of mould prevailed.

Without looking around, Meaulnes stretched himself out on the damp hay, elbow on the ground, head in hand. Having removed his belt, he curled up in his smock, his knees to his chest. Then he thought with regret of the mare's blanket which he had left on the path, and felt so miserable and so angry with himself that he wanted to weep.

He forced himself to think about something else. Frozen to the marrow, he remembered a dream – 'more of a vision' – that he had had as a child and about which he had never spoken to anyone. One day, instead of waking up in his room where his trousers and overcoat were hanging, he found himself in a long, green room with wall hangings like foliage. The room was filled with such a soft light that one could imagine it had a flavour. Near the window, a young girl was sewing, her back turned to him, seeming to be waiting for him to wake up . . . He did not have the energy to slip out of bed and walk around this enchanted dwelling. He fell asleep again, but next time, he swore to himself, he would get up. Tomorrow morning, perhaps . . .

CHAPTER XI

THE MYSTERIOUS DOMAIN

AT daybreak, he started walking again, but his swollen knee was so painful that he had to stop and sit from time to time. He had arrived in the most desolate place in the entire Sologne region, and all morning long he saw no one but a shepherdess on the distant horizon, bringing home her flock. He hailed her in vain, trying to run, but she disappeared without hearing him.

Even so, he continued to limp in her direction, distressingly slowly. Not a roof, not a soul, not even the cry of a curlew in the marsh reeds. This perfect solitude was illuminated by a bright, glacial December sun.

It must have been three o'clock in the afternoon when he finally caught sight of the top of a grey turret above the fir trees.

'Some old abandoned manor,' he said to himself, 'or a deserted dovecote . . .'

Without hurrying, he continued to walk. At the corner of the wood, between two posts, a path opened up. Meaulnes started down it. He took several steps and stopped, surprised and troubled by an inexplicable emotion. He pressed on, however, with the same tired footsteps, the icy wind chapping his lips and almost taking his breath away; nonetheless, an extraordinary contentment buoyed him up, a perfect almost intoxicating peace, a certainty that he was achieving his goal and pure happiness lay ahead. It was the same sensation he experienced in former years on the eve of summer festivals when at nightfall the town streets were decorated with fir trees, and the view from his bedroom window was obstructed by their branches.

'So much joy just because I'm reaching an old birdhouse, full of owls and draughts?'

Annoyed at himself, he stopped, wondering if it was not better to retrace his steps and continue on to the next village. While he was reflecting, head lowered, he suddenly noticed that the path had been swept in large circles, in the manner in which they were prepared for festivals back home. The road was like La Ferté's main street when the village was celebrating the Assumption! He could not have been more surprised had he seen a band of people in festive mood, raising dust the way they did in the month of June.

'Can there possibly be a festival here, in this lonely spot?' he wondered.

As he neared the first bend, he heard the sound of approaching voices. He jumped sideways into some dense young fir trees, crouched down, and listened, holding his breath. The voices were very young. A group of children passed close by him. One of them, probably a little girl, was talking in such a wise and knowing tone that Meaulnes could not refrain from smiling even though he could barely make out her words.

'Just one thing worries me,' she said, 'and that's the question of the horses. For example, we'll never keep Daniel from riding the big yellow pony.'

'No one can stop me,' replied a boy in a mocking voice. 'Don't we have permission to do whatever we want, even if it might hurt us?'

The voices moved away just as another group approached.

'If the ice has melted, we'll go by boat tomorrow morning,' said another little girl.

'But are we allowed to?' said another.

'We can organise the party any way we want.'

'But what happens if Frantz comes home this evening with his fiancée?'

'Well, he must do whatever we command!'

'This no doubt has something to do with a wedding,' said Augustin to himself. 'But do children make the laws here? What a strange place!'

He wanted to leave his hiding place and ask them where he could find something to eat and drink. He stood up and saw the last group going off in the distance, three little girls in straight, knee-length dresses. They wore pretty bridal headdresses, each with a curly, white plume. One of them, with her back to him, bent down to listen to her friend who, with her finger raised, was delivering some serious explanation.

'I would frighten them,' Meaulnes told himself, glancing at his ripped tunic and the crude belt worn by schoolboys at Sainte-Agathe.

Fearing that the children might run into him coming back along the avenue, he continued past the fir trees in the direction of the 'dovecote' without thinking too much about what he might find there. His way was soon blocked by a low, moss-covered wall at the edge of the woods. On the other side, between the wall and some outbuildings, was a long, narrow courtyard, jostling with carriages, like the courtyard of an inn on the day of a fair. The carriages came in all shapes and sizes: fine little four-seaters with their shafts in the air; charabancs; old-fashioned coaches with moulded roof racks; even ancient berlins with their windows shut.

Hidden behind the fir trees, for fear someone might catch sight of him, Meaulnes surveyed the confusion. He noticed on the other side of the courtyard, just above the seat in a high charabanc, a window half open in one of the outbuildings. Two iron bars, like those that keep stable shutters firmly closed, must have sealed off this entrance in the past, but time had broken them loose.

'I will climb in that window,' he said to himself. 'And sleep in the hay and leave at dawn without frightening those pretty little girls.'

He crawled over the wall, painfully because of his injured knee, and, passing from one carriage to another, from the seat of a charabanc to the roof of a berlin, he reached the level of the window. When he pushed, it opened like a door, and without a sound.

He found himself not in a hay loft but in a vast room with a low ceiling, which must have been a bedroom. In the low light of winter, he could see that the table, the mantelpiece, and even the armchairs were laden with large vases, valuable objects, and ancient weapons. At the far end of the room curtains hung to the floor, hiding what was probably an alcove.

Meaulnes closed the window, as much because of the cold as for fear of being observed from outside. He crossed to the other end of the room, lifted the curtains, and discovered a large, low bed, covered with gold-embossed books, lutes with broken strings, and candelabra thrown down pell-mell. He pushed all these items into the back of the alcove, and then lay down to rest a little and reflect on the strange adventure into which he had thrown himself.

The silence was profound. Only occasionally he heard the groan of the December wind.

Sprawled out like this, Meaulnes asked himself if, in spite of all the strange encounters, in spite of the children's voices in the avenue, in spite of the jostling carriages, he had not simply found an old, abandoned building in the middle of a lonely winter, just as he had originally thought. But it soon seemed to him that the wind was bearing towards him the sound of music distantly recalled, like a memory full of charm and regret. He was reminded of those times when his mother, still young, played the piano in their living room, in the waning afternoon, while without saying a word, he would hide behind the door that opened into the garden, and listen to her until night fell.

'Is someone, nearby, playing a piano?' he wondered.

But he left this question unanswered because he was over-whelmed by fatigue and soon fell asleep.

CHAPTER XII

WELLINGTON'S ROOM

IT was night when he awoke. Frozen to the marrow, he tossed and turned, rolling and crumpling his smock underneath him. A feeble, gloomy light shone on the alcove hangings.

He sat up and poked his head between the curtains. Someone had opened the window and attached two green Chinese lanterns to its frame.

Scarcely had Meaulnes glimpsed this when he heard the sound of muffled footsteps on the landing and a whispered conversation. He jerked back into the alcove, but his hob-nailed boots clanged against one of the bronze objects he had pushed against the wall. He held his breath. The footsteps approached and two shadows glided across the room.

'Don't make any noise,' said one.

'It's about time he woke up,' replied the other.

'Have you stocked up his room?'

'Yes, like the others'.'

The wind buffeted the open window.

'Hang on!' said the first. 'You haven't even shut the window, and the wind has already blown out one of the lanterns. You must relight it.'

'What's the point of lighting up the countryside, the wilderness?' asked the other, sounding lazy and discouraged. 'There's no one out there to see it.'

'What do you mean "no one"? More guests will be arriving during the course of the night. They will be very glad to see our lights from their carriages!'

Meaulnes heard the striking of a match. The man who had spoken last and who seemed to be the boss, said in a drawling voice, in the manner of one of Shakespeare's gravediggers:

'You've put green lanterns in Wellington's chamber. Why not red ones as well? You don't know what you're doing any more than I do.' Silence.

'. . . Wellington, he was an American, wasn't he? Is green an American colour? You, the well-travelled actor, should know that.'

'Ha! Well-travelled?' replied the other. 'Yes, I have travelled. But I have seen nothing. What can you see from inside a caravan?'

Meaulnes peered carefully between the curtains.

The man who was in charge was fat, bare-headed, and buried in the depths of an enormous overcoat. He held a long pole decorated with multicoloured lanterns. With one leg crossed over the other, he watched quietly while his companion worked.

As for the actor, he had the most pitiful body imaginable. Tall, skinny, trembling, glassy-eyed, and squinting, with a moustache straggling down over his toothless mouth, he made one think of a drowned man, streaming on a slab. He was shivering in his shirt-sleeves, and by word and gesture displayed his utter self-contempt.

After a moment of reflection that looked bitter and comical at the same time, he approached his partner, threw open his arms, and confided:

'You want me to tell you something? I can't understand why disgusting types like us were chosen to serve at a celebration like this. But there it is, old chap.'

Paying no attention to this heartfelt outburst, the fat man, still with his legs crossed, continued to watch his comrade work, yawned, and sniffed gently. Then, turning his back, he set off, pole on shoulder, saying:

'Let's go! It's time to dress for dinner.'

The actor followed him, but as he passed the alcove, he bowed and said mockingly:

'Mr Sleepyhead, all you have to do is to wake up and dress

yourself as a marquis, even if you are only a poor unfortunate like me. Then you must come to the fancy-dress party since this is the dearest wish of the little ladies and gentlemen.'

With a final bow, he added, in the patter of a fairground entertainer:

'Our companion, Maloyau, kitchen attaché, will play Harlequin, and I, your servant, the immortal Pierrot.'

CHAPTER XIII

THE STRANGE CELEBRATION

ONCE they had disappeared, Meaulnes left his hiding place. His feet were frozen, his joints stiff, but he was rested and his knee felt better.

'Dinner!' he thought. 'I can't miss this. I'll appear to be a guest whose name everyone has forgotten. Besides, I am not an intruder here because it's quite clear that Monsieur Maloyau and his companion were expecting me.'

Emerging from the total darkness of the alcove, he was able to survey the room by the light of the green lanterns.

The gypsy had fitted him out. Coats hung from coathooks. On a marble-topped table, he had supplied everything a fellow needed to transform himself from someone who had spent the preceding night in a sheepfold into a dandy. Matches sat on the mantelpiece next to a large flambeau. But no one had waxed the floor and Meaulnes was aware of rubble and sand crunching underfoot. Again he had the impression he was in a long-abandoned house. Going towards the fireplace, he bumped up against a pile of large cartons and little boxes. He reached out, lit a candle, opened the lids, and looked in.

Inside were clothes worn by young people long ago, frock-coats with high velvet collars, fine waistcoats, innumerable white ties, and patent-leather shoes dating from the beginning of the century. He did not dare touch anything, even with a fingertip, but after he had washed, shivering, he put one of the fine coats on over his smock. He raised its pleated collar, replaced his hob-nailed boots with shiny pumps and, bare-headed, set off down the stairs.

Without encountering anyone, he arrived at the foot of the

wooden staircase in a corner of the darkened courtyard. Night's icy breath blew on his face and lifted his coat-tails.

He took several steps and, thanks to some brightness in the sky, quickly became aware of the layout of the place. The courtyard was formed by outbuildings. Everything appeared old and derelict. Openings at the bottom of stairways gaped wide, long since lacking their doors. Windowpanes were missing, leaving black holes in the walls. Even so, all the buildings felt mysteriously festive, and the ground had been weeded and swept. Glittering colours flitted around in the lower rooms, where lanterns had also been lit on the side that faced the fields. Listening hard, Meaulnes thought he heard voices of little children and young girls coming from somewhere in the jumble of buildings where the wind shook branches in front of the pink, green, and blue of the glimmering windows.

Meaulnes was standing there in his big coat, half bent over, listening hard like a hunter, when a short, extraordinary-looking young man came out of a nearby building, which had appeared empty until then.

He wore a top hat with a flared crown, which shone like silver in the dark; a tailcoat whose collar rose up into his hair, an open waistcoat, and trousers held in place by straps that passed under his shoes. This dandy, who must have been about fifteen, walked on his toes as if he were pulled up by the elastic straps, but with extraordinary speed. Without stopping, he gave a deep, automatic bow to Meaulnes as he passed, and disappeared into the darkness towards the central building – farm, castle, abbey, or whatever it was – whose turret had guided Meaulnes at the beginning of the afternoon.

After a moment's hesitation, Meaulnes followed, hard on his heels. They crossed a formal garden, passed between two clumps of bushes, skirted a fishpond surrounded by a fence, and a well, and found themselves at last on the threshold of the central building.

A heavy wooden door, arched and studded like the door of a presbytery, was half open. The young dandy dived inside. Meaulnes followed him, and from the moment he set foot in the corridor, found himself surrounded by laughter, songs, calls and games of chase, even though he saw no one.

At the end of one corridor, another crossed it, and Meaulnes hesitated about whether to continue to the end of the first or to open one of the doors behind which he heard voices. Suddenly, two young girls materialised, chasing one another at the far end of the corridor. Soft-footed in his fine shoes, he ran to catch up with them. He heard the sound of doors opening, and saw two fifteen-year-old faces, rosy from the chase and the freshness of the evening, half-hidden under large bonnets, about to disappear in the sudden burst of light. For an instant, the girls spun around playfully, their light skirts lifting up, full of air, revealing the lace on their charming pantaloons. Then after their pirouette, they bounded back together into the room and shut the door.

Meaulnes remained in the dark corridor for a moment, dazzled and staggering. He was afraid of being caught, well aware that his hesitant, clumsy manner might mark him as a thief. Resolutely, he turned to leave, when once again he heard the sound of footsteps at the end of the corridor and the voices of children. Two little boys came towards him, chatting.

'Are we going to eat soon?' Meaulnes asked them, trying to sound confident.

'Come with us,' responded the bigger, 'we'll lead you there.'

With the trusting and friendly manner that children have just before a big party, each took him by a hand. They were probably two young peasants in their best clothes: breeches cut short at the knee, displaying heavy woollen stockings and clogs; tight little jerkins made of blue velour; caps of the same colour; and white ties.

'Do you know her?' asked one of the children.

'Mama told me that she will be wearing a black dress and a ruff and that she looks like a pretty pierrot,' said the smaller boy, who had a round head and innocent eyes.

'Who?' asked Meaulnes.

'The fiancée Frantz has gone to fetch.'

Before Meaulnes could speak, all three of them arrived at the door of a grand room where a fine fire was blazing. Planks resting on trestles served as tables, spread with white tablecloths. People of all sorts were seated at them, dining ceremoniously.

CHAPTER XIV

THE STRANGE CELEBRATION (CONTINUED)

IT was the kind of meal that is offered on the eve of a wedding to relations who have journeyed a long distance. The setting for this one was a large room with a low ceiling.

The two boys had let go of Meaulnes's hands and rushed into an adjoining room, from which young voices could be heard, and the clinking of spoons against plates. Without arousing suspicion, Meaulnes stepped over a bench and sat down next to two old peasant women. Fiercely hungry, he immediately started eating, only lifting his head after a while to survey the other guests and to listen to what they were saying.

No one spoke much, and it seemed that people hardly knew each other. Some must have come from the nearby countryside, others from distant towns. Interspersed along the length of the table were several ancient men, some with side whiskers and others shaved clean, who might have been old sailors. Near them dined other old men who closely resembled them: same tanned face, same lively eyes under bushy eybrows, same narrow ties like shoelaces. But it was easy to see that these men had never left the area. If they had pitched and rolled a thousand times in downpours and windstorms, it was on the tough but safe voyage, ploughing up and down their fields. Meaulnes saw hardly any women except for some old peasant ladies with round faces, like wrinkled apples, under frilly bonnets.

He felt completely at ease with these people, and explained this impression later: 'When you have committed an unpardonable wrong, you remember sometimes, in the hell of your bitterness, that there are certain people in the world who will always forgive you. You picture the old ones, the grandparents, full of kindness, who will always believe that everything you do is well done.' Most of the people at his table were this type; the rest were teenagers and young children.

The two old women next to Meaulnes were chatting to each other.

'Even if all goes well,' said the older, in a funny, high-pitched voice that she tried in vain to modulate, 'the engaged couple won't get here before three o'clock tomorrow.'

'Oh, hush! You're making me cross,' replied the other in a most calm tone. She wore a wide-brimmed bonnet.

'Let's add it up,' responded the first without budging. 'An hour and a half on the train from Bourges to Vierzon, and seven leagues by coach from Vierzon to here.'

The discussion continued, with Meaulnes absorbing every word. Thanks to their little disagreement, he formed some idea of the situation: Frantz de Galais, heir to the manor – a student or a sailor or marine cadet, no one knew – had gone to Bourges to find a young woman and to marry her. What was strange was that this boy, who must have been very young and very capricious, ruled the domain just as he pleased. He had demanded that the manor should resemble a festive palace for his fiancée's arrival, and he had invited all these children and good-natured old people to celebrate. And this is what the old women were discussing. Everything else remained a mystery, as they returned time and again to the question of when the couple would arrive. One thought it would happen the following morning; the other favoured the afternoon.

'My poor Moinelle, you're still as crazy as ever,' said the younger one calmly.

'And you, my poor Adèle, are as stubborn as ever. It's been four years since I last saw you, and you haven't changed in the least,' replied the other, shrugging her shoulders, but in her most peaceful voice.

They continued to snipe at each other without the slightest ill humour. Meaulnes interrupted them, hoping to learn more:

'Is Frantz's fiancée as pretty as they say?'

They looked at him, disconcerted. No one other than Frantz had seen the young woman, they declared. One evening on his way home from Toulon, he had come across her in a state of distress, in the Les Marais parks in Bourges. Her father, a weaver, had thrown her out of the house. She was extraordinarily pretty, and Frantz decided on the spot to marry her. It was a strange story, but hadn't the boy's father, Monsieur de Galais, and his sister Yvonne, always humoured his every whim?

Just as Meaulnes began cautiously asking a few more questions, a most attractive couple appeared in the doorway: a girl of sixteen in a velvet bodice and a skirt with deep flounces, and a young man in a high-collared tailcoat and trousers with braces. They danced across the room together; others followed them, while still more rushed past, running, squealing, pursued by a huge, pale pierrot, trailing his sleeves, wearing a black hat, and laughing from his toothless mouth.

He ran with clumsy strides, as if he wanted to leap up into the air with each step, and flapped his long, empty sleeves up and down. The young girls seemed scared of him, but the young men shook him by the hand, and the little children pursued him with piercing squeals, thrilled and delighted. As he passed Meaulnes, he gave him a glassy-eyed stare, and Meaulnes thought he recognised Maloyau's companion, now completely clean-shaven, the man who had strung up the lanterns.

Dinner was over. Everyone rose.

In the wide passages, people began dancing rounds and farandoles. Someone, somewhere, was playing a minuet. With his head half-hidden by the collar of his coat, as though it were a ruff, Meaulnes felt he was another person. Caught up in the fun, he too began pursuing the big pierrot through corridors that seemed like the wings of a theatre when the pantomime spills over from the stage. He became part of an extravagantly costumed, joyous crowd, late into the night. Sometimes he opened the door to a room where a lantern-slide show was in progress and children were applauding noisily. Other times, in the corner of a room where people were dancing, he would engage some young dandy in conversation, taking the opportunity to make enquiries about what costumes people would wear in the following days.

At length, uneasy about all the pleasure on offer and fearing every moment that his half-open coat would reveal his school uniform, he went to hide for a moment in the darkest, most peaceful part of the building, where he could hear nothing but the muffled sound of a piano.

He entered a silent room, a dining room, lit by an overhead light. Here too a party was going on, a party for little children. Some, seated on cushions on the floor, flicked through albums, open on their knees. Others were crouched on the ground in front of a chair, concentrating hard on laying out a display of pictures on its seat. Still others, near the fire, were saying nothing, doing nothing, except listening to the sound of celebration in the far reaches of the immense house.

One door of this dining room was wide open, and Meaulnes heard someone playing the piano in the adjoining room. Inquisitively, he poked his head through the door of what turned out to be a sort of small drawing room. With her back turned to him, a young woman, perhaps no more than a girl, with a maroon coat thrown over her shoulders, was softly playing airs and little songs. On the sofa next to her, six or seven little boys and girls were sitting in a row, listening, as pretty as a picture and as well behaved as children sometimes are late at night. Every so often, one of them, bracing himself with his wrists, rose, slid along the ground, and made for the dining room. Then one of the others, who had finished looking at the pictures, came and took his place.

In this room, after all the charming but feverish and crazy festivity, where even he had joined in the pursuit of the big pierrot, Meaulnes found himself plunged into the calmest kind of happiness in the world.

While the young woman continued to play, he returned to the

dining room and sat down without making a noise. Opening one of the big red albums spread out on the table, he began flipping through it absent-mindedly.

Almost immediately, one of the children jumped up from his spot on the floor, pulled on Meaulnes's arm, and hauled himself on to his lap so that he could see what Meaulnes was looking at. Another did the same on his other side. Meaulnes had a startling sensation of déjà vu: he had already dreamed about this moment. He was a married man in his own house on a beautiful evening, and the charming, unknown person playing the piano nearby was his wife.

CHAPTER XV

THE ENCOUNTER

MEAULNES was up bright and early the next morning. As advised, he dressed in a simple, black, old-fashioned costume with a jacket narrowed at the waist, sleeves puffed at the shoulders, a double-breasted waistcoat, trousers wide enough at the bottom to cover his fine shoes, and a top hat.

No one was about when he went downstairs. As he stepped into the courtyard, he felt that spring had arrived. It was an exceptionally mild day, and the sun was shining the way it does at the beginning of April. The frost had melted and the wet grass gleamed as if moistened by dew. Birds were singing in the trees, and from time to time a warm breeze wafted past Meaulnes's face.

He felt as guests do when they wake before their host. He kept expecting that at any moment a merry voice would call out to him in the courtyard: 'Already up, Augustin?'

But he walked by himself for a long time around the garden and the courtyard. Over in the main building, nothing stirred, neither at the windows nor in the turret. However, the rounded, wooden double doors were already open, and a ray of sun glinted off one of the high windows in the early-morning light.

For the first time, Meaulnes could examine the property by daylight. Vestiges of a wall separated the unkempt garden from the courtyard, where someone had recently spread and raked the sand. A jumble of stables with cracks and crannies sprouting wild brush and writhing vines stood at the far end of the outbuildings where he had slept. Fir trees surrounded the whole domain and hid the view of the lower land, except towards the east, where blue hills covered by rocks and still more fir trees came into view.

Meaulnes leaned for a while on the shaky, wooden fence surrounding the fishpond. Thin ice, crinkled like frozen foam, crusted its edges. He could see himself in his romantic costume, reflected in the water, as if he were leaning on the sky. This was a different Meaulnes, no longer the schoolboy who had escaped in a peasant's wagon, but a charming, romantic figure out of the pages of a beautiful, costly book.

His stomach growled, so he hurried over to the main building. In the large room where he had dined the night before, a peasant woman was setting the tables. After Meaulnes seated himself in front of one of the bowls set out on the tablecloth, she poured coffee for him, saying:

'You are the first, sir.'

He did not want to reply for fear of being recognised as a stranger. All he asked was what time the boat would leave for the proposed excursion that morning.

'Not for at least half an hour, sir. No one is up yet,' was the response.

Looking for the dock, he continued wandering around the exterior of the long manor house, which, with its uneven wings, resembled a church. As he rounded the south wing, he suddenly noticed reeds as far as the eye could see. Water lapped at the foot of the walls, and little woooden balconies overhung the marsh.

Meaulnes roamed idly along the sandy bank, which was like a towpath, peering through the dusty glass panes of tall doors that opened into abandoned rooms cluttered with wheelbarrows, rusty tools, and broken flower pots. Suddenly, from the other end of the buildings, he heard footsteps crunching on the sand.

It was two women, one very old and bent, the other young, blonde, and slender, whose charming outfit seemed extraordinarily out of place to Meaulnes after all the fantastic costumes of the previous evening. The two stopped for a moment to admire the landscape while Meaulnes told himself, with an amazement which later seemed extremely crude:

'Here without doubt is what is called an eccentric young woman – perhaps an actress summoned for the occasion.'

They passed near where Meaulnes was standing stock-still, giving him an opportunity to take a good look at the younger one. Often, later, as he was falling asleep, desperately trying to recall her beautiful face, he saw in his dreams row upon row of young women who all looked like her. One wore a hat like hers; another had her slightly bent head; one had her pure gaze; another had her narrow waist; and another, the same blue eyes. But none of them perfectly resembled the tall young woman.

Meaulnes had time to notice her luxuriant, fair hair and her neat features, almost poignant in their delicacy. All too soon, she had passed by, but he continued to admire her dress from the back, and found it to be the simplest, most sensible of garments.

Should he follow them? he was wondering, when the young woman spoke to her companion, while turning imperceptibly towards him:

'I think the boat will be here soon.'

Meaulnes followed them. Even though the old lady was bent and shaky, she never stopped chatting and laughing, and the young woman responded sweetly. And when they went down on to the dock, she had that same innocent, serious look, which seemed to say to him:

'Who are you? What are you doing here? I don't know you, do I?'

By this time, other guests were scattered among the trees, waiting. Three pleasure boats drew up alongside the dock, ready to receive passengers. One by one, as the two women – surely the lady of the manor and her daughter? – passed by, the young men bowed deeply and the young women curtsied. What a strange morning! What a peculiar party! In spite of the winter sun, it was cold, and the women wrapped fashionable feather boas around their necks.

The old lady remained ashore, and without knowing quite how

it happened, Meaulnes found he was in the same boat as the daughter of the manor. He stood on deck, holding on to his wind-whipped hat with one hand and leaning forward so he could keep an eye on her. She had found a sheltered spot and was watching him too. She would respond to her companions with a smile, and then turn her blue eyes sweetly on him, gently biting her lip.

Silence reigned on the nearby banks, and the boat flew past with the soothing rumble of an engine churning through water. It felt like midsummer, as though they might disembark at a country house with a beautiful garden. There the young girl would walk up and down, under a white parasol. Doves would coo until night fell. But suddenly a frigid gust of wind reminded the revellers at this strange celebration that it was still December.

They disembarked beside a wood of fir trees. The passengers had to wait a moment on the pier, bunched up against each other, while one of the boatmen opened the padlock to the gate. Meaulnes later recalled, with great emotion, the exact instant, as he was standing at the edge of the lake, that he gazed at the face of the young woman he would soon lose. He stared so hard at this exquisite profile that his eyes welled up with tears. He remembered noticing a little bit of powder resting on her cheek, like a delicate secret she was confiding to him.

On land, everything took on a dreamlike quality. While the children ran around, hooting with joy, and groups formed and scattered throughout the woods, Meaulnes took the path where the young woman was walking a few steps ahead of him. When he caught up with her, he blurted out:

'You are beautiful.'

But she hurried on without replying, and disappeared down a side path. Other walkers rushed past, playing games, wandering as they pleased, led along by pure fantasy. Meaulnes reproached himself sharply for what he felt was his clumsiness, his crudeness, his stupidity. He rambled around aimlessly, convinced he would never see the graceful creature again. But suddenly he caught sight of her coming in his direction, forced to pass close by him on the narrow path. With her lovely, bare hands she was folding back her overcoat. On her feet, she wore very skimpy black shoes, and her ankles were so narrow that when she flexed them, it seemed they might snap.

This time Meaulnes greeted her, and said softly:

'Please forgive me.'

'I forgive you,' she said seriously. 'But I must rejoin the children since they are in charge today. Goodbye.'

Augustin begged her to stay a moment longer. His plea was awkward, but his words were so troubled and full of confusion that she slowed down and listened to him.

'I don't even know who you are,' she said at last.

She spoke firmly, but her voice softened a little when she came to the last word. Then her blue eyes looked straight ahead, her face resumed its fixed look, and she chewed her lip.

'I don't know your name either,' replied Meaulnes.

They were following an open road and saw some of the guests in the distance gathering around a house that stood all alone in the middle of the countryside.

'There's Frantz's house,' said the young woman. 'I must leave you.'

She hesitated, looked at him with a smile, and introduced herself:

'My name? I am Mademoiselle Yvonne de Galais.'

And then she vanished.

No one lived in Frantz's house, but even so Meaulnes found it crammed to the rafters with a crowd of revellers. He had no time to examine the place; everyone was hurriedly eating the cold lunch, brought along in the boats and quite at odds with the season – no doubt the children had chosen the menu. When he noticed Mademoiselle de Galais preparing to leave, he approached her and returned to their earlier conversation.

'The name I gave you was even more beautiful.'

'Really! What was it?' she asked, with the same seriousness.

But he was worried that he might have said something silly, and took a different tack.

'My name is Augustin Meaulnes,' he continued, 'and I am a student.'

'Oh. You study?' she said. And they conversed a little longer, slowly, happily – in a friendly way. Then the young woman's expression changed again. Less haughty and less serious now, she also appeared more anxious, and wary about what Meaulnes might say. Beside him she trembled like a swallow which had landed for a instant but was already shivering with desire to fly off again.

Whenever Meaulnes suggested something they might do together, she countered:

'What's the point? What's the point?'

But when at last he screwed up enough courage to ask her permission to return to her beautiful domain one day, she replied quite simply:

'I will wait for you.'

At the dock, she stopped abruptly and reflected.

'We are two children, and this is madness. We must not go back in the same boat. Goodbye. Don't follow me.'

Meaulnes was stunned as he watched her leave. Then he began walking again. In the distance, she stopped and turned towards him just before disappearing into the crowd. For the first time she gazed at him at length. Was this a last farewell? Was this a message to prevent him from accompanying her? Or did she have something more she wanted to say to him?

After everyone had returned to the manor, the pony races began in a large, sloping meadow behind the farm. This was the final part of the festivities. Everyone agreed that the engaged couple would probably arrive in good time for the races because Frantz was in charge of them.

All the same, they began without him. Some boys in jockey

outfits and girls in riding habits led out high-spirited, beribboned ponies, while others led out docile, older horses. With all the shouting and laughter, the bets and loud ringing of the bell, Meaulnes felt he had been transported to a well-tended, miniature racecourse.

He recognised Daniel and the little girls with plumed hats whom he had encountered the evening before. So anxious was he to find a charming rose-covered hat and maroon greatcoat in the crowd that the rest of the spectacle escaped him. But Mademoiselle de Galais did not appear. He was still looking for her when a ringing of bells and joyous cries announced the end of the race. The victor was a little girl on an old grey mare, and she rode past triumphantly, the feather in her hat floating in the wind.

Suddenly everyting went silent. The games were over and Frantz had still not arrived. Everyone hung around for a while, worriedly consulting each other. At last, in little groups, they retired to their lodgings, anxiously, silently, awaiting the arrival of Frantz and his fiancée.

CHAPTER XVI

FRANTZ DE GALAIS

THE races had finished too early. It was half past four, still daylight, when Meaulnes returned to his room, his head full of the events of that extraordinary day. He sat down at the table, idle, waiting for dinner and the festivities which would follow.

The same wild wind was blowing that had blown the previous evening. It roared and whooshed like a waterfall. The fireplace flue-shutter banged now and again.

For the first time, Meaulnes felt the kind of anxiety that takes hold at the end of a day which has been too wonderful. He thought about lighting the fire, but tried in vain to lift the rusty shutter. Then he started tidying the room, hanging his beautiful outfits on the coat-rack, arranging the overturned chairs neatly along the wall, as though he were preparing for a long stay.

However, thinking that he should be ready to leave at any moment, he carefully folded his smock and the rest of his school clothes over the back of a chair – they would be his travelling outfit. Under the chair, he placed his hobnailed boots, still covered in mud, and sat down again to look around, calmer now because his den was neat.

From time to time, a drop of rain striped down the window which overlooked the coachyard and the fir trees. At peace, now that everything was in order, Meaulnes felt completely happy. There he was, a mysterious stranger, in the middle of an unfamiliar world, in a room of his choice. The experience up to this point had exceeded his wildest expectations. His joy was complete with the memory of the young woman's face turning towards him, radiant in the high wind.

During this reverie, night fell without his even thinking of lighting the torches. A gust of wind slammed open the door of the back bedroom which joined his and whose window also looked out on the coachyard. Meaulnes was going to shut the door when he noticed a light – a candle? – burning on the table in the other room. He put his head through the half-open door. Someone had entered the room, probably through the window, and was walking softly up and down. As far as he could discern, it was a young man. Bare-headed, with a traveller's cape over his shoulders, he walked to and fro, as if maddened by unbearable sadness. The wind from the open window made his cape flap, and each time he passed near the light, Meaulnes could see the gleam of the gilt buttons on his fine frock-coat.

He whistled something through his teeth, a sort of sea shanty, the kind of song sailors and girls sing in cabarets on the docks, to lift their spirits. In the middle of his anxious walking, he stopped abruptly and leaned over the table, peered into a box, and took out a sheaf of papers. By the light of the candle, Meaulnes saw a fine profile, aquiline, clean-shaven, under thick hair parted on the side. The young man stopped whistling. Very pale, his lips half open, he seemed out of breath, as if he had received a violent blow to his chest.

Meaulnes hesitated, wondering whether to retire discreetly or to move forward and place a friendly hand on his shoulder and talk to him. But the young man lifted his head and saw him. He looked Meaulnes over, and then without showing surprise approached him and said in a firm voice:

'I do not know you, sir, but I am happy to see you. Since you are here at this very moment, you will be the one to hear my explanation . . . So, here goes . . .'

He seemed to be completely distraught. As he said 'Here goes,' he took Meaulnes by the lapels to hold his attention. Then he looked towards the window, as though planning what to say. He squeezed his eyes shut, and Meaulnes realised he was on the verge of tears. Choking back a sob, and still looking fixedly at the window, he began again in a changed voice.

'Well. That's it. The festivities are over. You can go down and tell them I have returned alone. My fiancée will not be coming. On principle, out of fear, or from a lack of faith? Anyway, sir, I shall try to explain.'

But he could not continue. His whole face crumpled, and he explained nothing. Suddenly, turning away into the shadows, he began opening and closing drawers full of clothes and books.

'I'm going to get ready to leave again,' he said. 'No one must disturb me.'

He placed various objects on the table, a sponge bag, and a pistol . . .

Meaulnes left in utter confusion, without daring to say a word to him or shake his hand.

Downstairs, a premonition that something had gone badly wrong hung in the air. Almost all the girls had changed their dresses. In the main building, dinner had commenced, but in the commotion, the diners were gobbling down their food in their haste to leave.

Various people rushed back and forth from the large kitchen-dining room to the upper rooms and to the stables, while others gathered in groups to say farewell to each other.

'What's happening?' Meaulnes asked one of the country boys who was hurrying to finish his meal, felt hat on head and napkin tucked into waistcoat.

'We're leaving,' the lad responded. 'A sudden decision. At five o'clock, all of us guests were standing around. We had waited until the very last minute, until there was no chance of the fiancée showing up. Someone said, "What if we left?" And everyone got ready to set off.'

Meaulnes did not reply. He did not mind leaving now. Wasn't this the end of the adventure for the moment? Hadn't he obtained

71

everything he desired this time? What he needed now was some peace in which to revisit the morning's wonderful conversation. It was time to leave, but he would return soon, this time without subterfuge.

'If you want to come with us,' continued the boy, who was about his age, 'hurry up and get ready. We'll hitch up shortly.'

Meaulnes rushed off, leaving behind the remains of his meal and neglecting to tell the other guests what he knew. The park, the garden, and the courtyard were sunk in darkness. No lanterns shone at the windows that evening. But because the dinner was the final meal after what should have been a wedding, the least reputable guests, fortified no doubt by wine, began singing. As Meaulnes drew further away, he could hear their bawdy songs rising up in the park which for two days had been the home of so much grace and so many marvels. This was the beginning of the havoc that followed. He passed by the fishpond where just that morning he had gazed at his reflection. How different everything seemed already, how changed by the snippets of this song and its bawdy chorus:

> *Where are you returning from, little libertine?*
> > *Your bonnet is torn*
> > *Your hair is a mess . . .*

It came again:

> > *My shoes are red . . .*
> > *Goodbye, my loves . . .*
> > *My shoes are red . . .*
> > *Goodbye for ever!*

As he arrived at the foot of the stairway to his isolated lodging, he collided with someone coming downstairs.

'Goodbye,' said a voice, and a figure wrapping himself up in a cape flitted past. It was Frantz de Galais.

Frantz had left a candle in his room, and it was still burning. Nothing was out of order. The only evidence of his visit was a piece of paper with these words:

> *My fiancée has disappeared, insisting that she cannot be my wife and informing me that she is a seamstress not a princess. I do not know what to do, so I am leaving. I no longer wish to live. I hope that Yvonne will forgive me for not saying goodbye, but she can do nothing for me now.*

The candle had nearly burned out, the flame flickered, sank, and died. Meaulnes returned to his own room and shut the door. In spite of the dark, he was able to make out all the objects he had so happily tidied up earlier in the day. Garment by garment, he gathered up his miserable old clothes, his boots, and heavy belt with brass buckle. He changed quickly, and placed the borrowed garments over a chair, leaving behind the wrong waistcoat by mistake.

Under the windows, in the coachyard, chaos reigned. People were pulling, shouting, and shoving, each wanting to free his conveyance from the inextricable jam. From time to time, a man climbed on the seat of a coach or on to the roof of a large carriage, and turned on his lantern, so that light poured through Meaulnes's window, and for a moment, he believed he saw the familiar surroundings twitch and come to life.

And so he left the mysterious place he might never see again, closing the door firmly behind him.

CHAPTER XVII

THE STRANGE CELEBRATION (FINALE)

ALREADY a line of coaches was rolling slowly through the night towards the gateway to the woods. At its head, a man in a goatskin coat, holding a lantern, led the first team's horse by its bridle.

Meaulnes scurried around, trying to find a lift, desperate to leave and deeply concerned he might suddenly find himself alone at the manor house, his ruse uncovered. In front of the main building, the drivers were sorting out loads for the last carriages. Passengers had to stand while the seats were adjusted. The young girls stood with difficulty, all bundled up as they were, wraps falling to their feet, faces anxious in the lantern light as they bent their heads.

Meaulnes recognised one of the coach drivers. It was the young peasant boy who, earlier, had offered him a lift.

'May I come along?' Meaulnes cried out.

'Where are you going?' replied the other, clearly not recognising him in return.

'Near Sainte-Agathe.'

'Ask Maritain for a seat.'

Meaulnes began searching for the unknown Maritain in the sea of delayed travellers. Someone pointed him out where he sat singing loudly among the drinkers in the kitchen.

Meaulnes thought about the anxious young woman, nervous and saddened, who would have to listen to the caterwauling of these wine-soaked louts all night. Where was her room? Where was her window among all these mysterious buildings? But he had nothing to gain by waiting. He had to leave. Once back in Sainte-Agathe, everything would become clear. No longer a truant schoolboy, he would have a chance to think about the daughter of the manor once again.

One by one the carriages departed, their wheels crunching on the sand of the main avenue. They turned and disappeared into the night, full of warmly wrapped women, with children muffled up in their scarves, already falling asleep. One more large cart passed by, one more charabanc with women squeezed in shoulder to shoulder, leaving Meaulnes standing on the threshold of the manor house. The only vehicle remaining was an old berlin, driven by a man in a peasant's smock.

'Come aboard,' he replied to Augustin's explanation of where he wanted to go, 'we're going in your direction.'

Meaulnes opened the door of the ancient vehicle with difficulty, its glass shaking and its hinges squealing. Two tiny children, a boy and a girl, were curled up asleep on a seat in a corner of the coach, but the noise and the cold air woke them. They uncurled, looked around vaguely, then, shivering, snuggled back into their corner and went to sleep again.

The coach creaked forward. Meaulnes shut the door with care, and installed himself in the other corner seat. Looking through the window, he forced himself to engrave on his memory the places he was leaving and the road by which he had arrived. In spite of the dark, he could see that the coach was crossing the courtyard and the garden, passing in front of the stairway to his room, going through the gateway, leaving the estate, and entering the woods. He vaguely made out the trunks of trees as they passed.

'Perhaps we will catch up with Frantz de Galais,' Meaulnes muttered to himself, his heart beating hard.

Abruptly, the carriage pulled to one side of the narrow road to avoid an obstacle, a massive, dark shape. It was a caravan almost in the middle of the road, parked there to be near the previous days' festivities.

Having navigated around this hazard, the horses set off again at a trot. Meaulnes was beginning to tire of straining through the window to pierce the surrounding darkness when a sudden flash burst out from the woods, followed by an explosion. The horses took off at a gallop. Whether the driver was trying to hold them back or urge them onwards, Meaulnes could not guess. He wanted to open the coach door, but the handle was on the outside and he tried in vain to lower the window, rattling it frantically. The children woke up, and clutched each other, speechless with terror. Meaulnes kept on shaking the window, his nose pressed against the pane, and glimpsed a white figure fleeing round a bend in the road. It was the tall Pierrot from the festivities, still in fancy dress, looking frantic and panic-stricken, gripping a body closely to his chest.

And then there was nothing.

The carriage rumbled through the night as fast as it could. The two children had fallen asleep again, and Meaulnes had no one with whom to discuss the mysterious events of the previous two days. He went over and over in his mind all that he had seen and heard. Finally, exhausted and heavy-hearted, he abandoned himself to sleep, like an unhappy child.

Dawn had not yet broken when the coach slowed down. Meaulnes was awakened by a knock on the window. The driver opened the door with difficulty, letting in the frigid night wind and chilling Meaulnes to the marrow.

'You must get off here. It's daybreak,' he yelled. 'We are setting off in a different direction now, and you are very near Sainte-Agathe.'

Stiff from being crammed in the corner, Meaulnes obeyed, automatically feeling around for his cap which had slid under the children's feet in the darkest corner of the coach. Then he climbed down.

'Goodbye,' said the coachman, climbing back up to his seat. 'You have only six kilometres to go. The milestone is there, at the edge of the road.'

Still half asleep, Meaulnes stumbled heavily towards the milestone

and sat down on it, his arms folded and his head lowered as if to go
back to sleep.

'Oh, no!' cried the coachman. 'You mustn't go to sleep there. Do
you want to freeze to death? Come on. Get up. Walk around a bit.'

Swaying like a drunkard, Meaulnes set off slowly down the road
towards Sainte-Agathe, his hands in his pockets, his shoulders
hunched, while the old berlin, that last remnant of his mysterious
adventure, swerved off the gravelled road and jolted silently away
down a grassy shortcut. The last Meaulnes saw of it was the driver's
hat dancing along above the hedges.

PART II

CHAPTER I

THE GREAT GAME

THE strong, cold wind; the rain or the snow; the impossibility of conducting serious reconnaisance; everything prevented Meaulnes and me from discussing the lost domain again before the end of winter. We could not start on anything serious during those short February Thursdays, with winds gusting back and forth, followed at about five o'clock by dreary, freezing rain.

Nothing at school reminded us of Meaulnes's adventure except the strange fact that, from the afternoon of his return, we no longer seemed to have any friends. During recreation time, the usual games were organised, but Jasmin no longer spoke to Meaulnes. In the evening, as soon as the classroom had been swept, the schoolyard emptied the way it had done when I was alone, and I would watch my companion wandering from the garden to the shed to the schoolyard to the dining room.

On Thursday mornings, we installed ourselves at desks in one of the two classrooms, and read books by Rousseau and Paul-Louis Courier that we dug out of cupboards where they had been stuck between English textbooks and carefully copied musical scores. On Thursday afternoons, if my mother had a visitor, we left the apartment and went back into the school. Sometimes we heard groups of older students stopping for a moment in front of the main entrance, as if by chance, crashing into it in some kind of incomprehensible military game, and then leaving.

This dull life continued until the end of February. I was starting to believe that Meaulnes had forgotten everything when a strange event proved me wrong. A serious crisis was boiling under the gloomy surface of our winter life.

It was actually on a Thursday evening towards the end of the month that the first piece of news from the strange domain came to us, the first intimation of adventure. It was late in the evening. My grandparents had left, and only Millie and my father were with us. Little did they know the reason for the silent hostility which had divided the class into two clans.

At eight o'clock, Millie opened the door to toss out some crumbs from our meal and said: 'Ah!' in such a surprised voice that we went to see what had happened. A blanket of snow lay on the doorstep. It was completely dark outside, but I took a few steps into the schoolyard to see how deep the snow was. I felt soft flakes drifting onto my face and then immediately melting. Millie pulled me in again sharply and shut the door against the cold.

By nine o'clock we were preparing to go up to bed. My mother already had the lamp in her hand when we clearly heard two heavy blows on the gate at the other end of the schoolyard. She put the lamp back on the table, and we stood frozen to the spot, listening hard.

It would have been stupid to go outside to see what had happened. The wind would blow out the lamp and might even break the glass before we were halfway across the yard. After a short silence, my father began to say, 'It was probably only . . .' when from just under the dining-room window, which looked out on to the station road (as I mentioned earlier), came a strident and prolonged whistle, loud enough to be heard as far away as the church. The whistle was immediately followed by piercing cries outside the windows from some partly hidden boys who had pulled themselves up on to the sill by their hands.

'Bring him out! Bring him out!' they yelled.

More cries came from the other end of the building. This group must have come via old Martin's field and climbed over the low wall that separated the field from our schoolyard.

From every direction, eight or ten unfamiliar, probably disguised, voices yelled one after the other, 'Bring him out!' The sound exploded from the storeroom roof, which they must have reached by climbing on a pile of logs that leaned against the exterior; from the low wall, between the shed and the gate, whose rounded top allowed a rider to mount a horse without difficulty; from the wall alongside the station road fence, easy enough to climb. Late arriving reinforcements entered the garden by the back gate, and they too joined in the racket, yelling, 'Let's take 'em on!'

They forced open the windows, and their cries echoed through the empty classrooms.

Meaulnes and I knew every twist and turn of the main building, and could visualise quite effectively on a mental map every position from which these invaders were attacking. Frankly, it was only in the first instant that we felt any fear, the moment when the whistle made all four of us think it was an attack by prowlers or gypsies. Indeed, a large, bandit-like person had been hanging around the square behind the church for a fortnight, accompanied by a young boy with his head swathed in bandages; and other strangers, also recently arrived in the district, were seeking employment with our blacksmiths and wheelwrights.

But from the moment we heard the assailants' cries, we felt convinced that we were dealing with locals, probably young men, although we could tell by some high-pitched voices that little boys were also part of the group invading our home as if they were boarding a ship.

'Good heavens!' cried my father, and Millie asked under her breath, 'What on earth does this mean?' and then suddenly, everywhere – at the entrance, on the fence, and outside the window – the yelling stopped. Two sharp whistles pierced the air beyond the casement, and the cries in the garden and from the top of the shed diminished steadily and then ceased. The whole troop gathered together and we could hear them brushing against the length of the dining-room wall as they beat a hasty retreat, the snow muffling the sound of their footsteps.

Someone had clearly disturbed them. At the time of night when everyone is usually asleep, they thought themselves safe to launch their attack on our isolated house on the outskirts of the village. But their plan of campaign had been disrupted.

The attack had been as sudden as a well-executed pirate assault on a ship. We had only just gathered our senses and gone outside when we heard a familiar voice cry out through the gate, 'Monsieur Seurel! Monsieur Seurel!'

It was Monsieur Pasquier, the butcher. The fat little man wiped his clogs on the doorstep, shook the snow from his short smock, and came inside. He looked shifty and alarmed, like someone who has just uncovered the entire secret of a mystery.

'I was in my courtyard, facing Four-Roads Square. I was on my way to shut the goat shed when, all of a sudden, what do I see standing up in the snow? Two big lads on the lookout, waiting for something. They were near the cross. I moved forwards two steps, and pouf! Off they went at the gallop towards your place. Me, I didn't hesitate. I picked up my lantern and said to myself, "I'll go and tell Monsieur Seurel about this."'

And he started his story all over again.

'I was in the courtyard behind my house . . .' At this, we offered him a liqueur, which he accepted, and asked him for some details, which he was incapable of providing.

He had seen nothing on his arrival at the house. All the troops, alerted by the two sentinels he had disturbed, vanished immediately. As to those two lookouts on horseback, 'They could have been gypsies,' he suggested. 'They've been around for nearly a month, waiting for good weather to put on a show. I wouldn't put it past them to have planned some kind of mischief.'

This did not move us much further along, and we remained standing, perplexed, while the man sipped his liqueur and went over his story again. Meaulnes, who had listened attentively up to that point, picked up the butcher's lamp and said firmly, 'We must go and see.'

He opened the door, and we followed him outside, my father, Monsieur Pasquier, and myself. Millie was reassured by the attackers' departure and, having very little natural curiosity, like most meticulously tidy people, declared:

'Go if you wish. But shut the door and take the key. I'm off to bed. I'll leave the lamp burning for your return.'

CHAPTER II

WE ARE AMBUSHED

WE set off across the snow in absolute silence. Meaulnes marched in front, projecting a fan of light through the open panel of the dark-lantern. We had just left the main entrance when two hooded individuals flew out, like surprised partridges, from behind the municipal see-saw close to our playground wall. Whether from mockery or pleasure caused by the strange game they were playing or excitement or fear of being overtaken, they jeered a few words at us as they ran away laughing.

Meaulnes dropped the lantern in the snow and cried out: 'Follow me, François!'

The two older men could not keep up with us, so we left them and launched ourselves in pursuit of the two shadows who, having just skirted the end of the village along the Vieille-Planche road, deliberately came back towards the church. They ran steadily, not too fast, and it was easy to follow them. They crossed the church street, where everything was silent, sleeping, and set off behind the cemetery into a maze of little alleys and dead ends.

This was the quarter known as Little Corners, where the day-labourers, dressmakers, and weavers lived. We did not know it well, and we had never been there at night. The place was deserted during the day, the labourers at work and the weavers confined indoors. During the vast, quiet night, it seemed more abandoned, more asleep than any other part of town. There was no chance of anyone showing up unexpectedly and lending us a hand.

I knew just one alley between the houses set down at random like so many cardboard boxes. It led to the home of the dressmaker nicknamed 'The Mute'. First we descended a steepish slope, paved in places, and after having made two or three turns between small courtyards and empty stables, we arrived at a complete dead end, closed in by a long-abandoned farmyard. On previous visits to The Mute's house, while she engaged my mother in silent conversation, wiggling her fingers and interjecting impotent squeaks, I would look through her casement window over the big wall of that farm, the last building on this side of town. The gate to the farmyard was always closed. The place was empty — not even a blade of straw — and nothing ever happened there.

This was precisely the road the two unknown fellows were following. We were frightened of losing them at each turn, but to my surprise we always arrived at the entrance to an alley just as they were leaving it. I say 'to my surprise' because these alleys were so short, and it would have been impossible to see them unless they slowed down each time we were about to lose them.

At last, they turned unhesitatingly down the street which led to The Mute's house, and I cried out to Meaulnes, 'We have them. It's a dead end!'

In truth, they had us. They had led us precisely where they wanted. Arriving at the wall, they turned towards us and one of them gave the same whistle we had already heard twice that evening.

Immediately, ten youths, lying in wait in the abandoned farmyard, sprang forward. They were all hooded, and their faces were covered by scarves.

Even so, we could tell who they were, and it was up to us to deal with them. We had already resolved to reveal nothing to Monsieur Seurel. Delouche, Denis, Giraudat, and all the others were there. In the struggle, we had recognised their method of fighting and their broken voices. But one issue remained disturbing and seemed to almost frighten. We did not recognise one of the gang, and he seemed to be the leader . . .

He did not touch Meaulnes. He watched his troops in their

tattered clothes, struggling in the snow, as they hounded my tall, breathless companion. Two of them took me on, immobilising me with difficulty because I fought like a devil. I was on the ground, knees bent, sitting on my heels, with my arms pinned together behind. I watched the scene unfold with intense, fearful curiosity.

Meaulnes had already shaken off four of our schoolmates, whom he detached from his smock by turning swiftly on himself and flinging them down into the snow. The unknown person, standing tall on both feet, calmly followed the battle with interest, repeating from time to time in a sharp voice, 'Keep going. Courage. Come back here. Go, go, go!'

He was clearly in command. Where had he come from? Where and how had he trained them for battle? This remained a mystery. His face was wrapped in a scarf, like the others, but when Meaulnes, now free of his adversaries, advanced towards him menacingly, he moved in order to assess the situation more clearly, and revealed a piece of white linen wound around his head like a bandage.

That is when I yelled at Meaulnes, 'Watch your back. There's another one.'

Meaulnes had no time to turn before a huge thug rose up from the gate behind him, deftly slipped a scarf around his neck and dragged him backwards. Immediately the four attackers Meaulnes had tossed into the snow joined in and immobilised his arms and legs by tying them with a rope and a scarf respectively. The youth with the bandaged head dug around in Meaulnes's pockets. The last arrival, a fellow with a lasso, lit a small candle which he protected with his hand. Each time the leader found a piece of paper in a pocket, he used this little light to examine its contents.

'This time we've got him! Here's the map! Here's the guide! Let's see if this gentleman really did go where I thought.'

His acolyte blew out the candle. The others picked up their caps and belts, and disappeared as silently as they had arrived, leaving me free to untie my companion as fast as I could.

'He won't get very far with that map,' said Meaulnes, standing up.

We set off again slowly because he was limping slightly, and met up again with Monsieur Seurel and Old Man Pasquier on Church Street.

'You haven't seen anything?' they asked. 'Neither have we.'

Thanks to the profound dark of the night, they had seen nothing. The butcher left us, and Monsieur Seurel hurried home to bed.

But we two, upstairs in our room, spent most of the night repairing our tattered clothes by the light of the lamp that Millie had left burning. In low voices we discussed what had happened to us, like two companions-in-arms on the night of a severe defeat.

CHAPTER III

THE GYPSY AT SCHOOL

WAKING up the next morning was painful. At half past eight, at the moment when Monsieur Seurel was about to give the signal to enter the school, Meaulnes and I arrived to join the queue, completely out of breath. Because we were late, we had to slip in anywhere; usually Meaulnes was first in the long line of students standing elbow to elbow, laden with textbooks, notebooks, and pens, that Monsieur Seurel inspected.

I was surprised by the silent willingness with which we were admitted into the middle of the line. While Monsieur Seurel scrutinised Meaulnes, holding back our entry for a few seconds, I stuck my head out curiously, looking left and right for the faces of our enemies from the previous evening.

The first I recognised was the one I had been thinking about all night, but the last I expected to see in this place. He stood in Meaulnes's usual place, right at the front, with one foot on the stone step and his shoulder and a corner of his knapsack propped against the door frame. He inclined his narrow face, very pale but slightly freckled, towards us with a smirk of disdainful curiosity. His head and one side of his face were covered with a white linen bandage. It was the ringleader, the young gypsy who had ambushed us the previous night.

But we were already filing into the classroom and taking our seats. The new student sat down beside the pillar at the left end of the long bench of which Meaulnes occupied the extreme right end. Giraudat, Delouche and the three others on this bench were

90

crowded together to make room for him, as if everything had been agreed in advance.

It often happened this way in winter – students would appear among us by chance, bargees held up by ice in the canals, apprentices, snowbound travellers. They stayed for a couple of days, a month, rarely longer. Objects of curiosity at first, they soon blended in with the crowd of regular students.

But this one would not be easily forgotten. I still remember this singular being and all the peculiar treasures he carried in his knapsack. First were the 'picture' nib holders, which he pulled out to write his dictation. If you shut one eye and looked through a hole in the shaft, an image appeared, blurred and magnified – the basilica at Lourdes or some other unknown monument. He chose one for himself, and the others passed from hand to hand. Then there was the Chinese pencil box holding a pair of compasses and other entertaining instruments. He sent these down the line, and the students moved them along from one to another under their note books so that Monsieur Seurel would see nothing.

He also passed out brand-new books, whose titles I had read longingly on the covers of the few books in our library: *La Teppe aux Merles, La Roche aux Mouettes, Mon Ami Benoist*. Who knows where these copies came from? Stolen perhaps? Some of us flicked through the volumes on our knees with one hand, while writing dictation with the other. Some twirled the compasses around on the interior of their desks. Some closed one eye and glued the other to a blurry and scratched view of Notre-Dame de Paris, while Monsieur Seurel, with his back turned, walked back and forth from his desk to the window, still dictating. The stranger, pen in hand and fine profile outlined against the grey pillar, winked at us, delighted with the furtive game he had organised.

But little by little, the pupils grew nervous as the objects being passed around all eventually arrived in Meaulnes's hands. Casually, without even a glance, he placed them beside him until he had assembled quite a pile, rather like the heap of objects that lie at the feet of Science in allegorical compositions. It was inevitable that Monsieur Seurel would discover this strange display and notice our little game. Besides, he must have been thinking about holding an enquiry into the previous night's events, and the gypsy's presence would make his task easier. And indeed, he soon stopped in surprise in front of Meaulnes.

'To whom does all this belong?' he asked, pointing to 'all this' with the back of his book closed over his index finger.

'I haven't the faintest idea,' said Meaulnes in a surly tone, without lifting his head.

But the stranger intervened.

'It's mine,' he said, adding quickly – with the elegant, sweeping gesture of a young squire, irresistible to the old teacher – 'I put it all at your disposal, sir, if you'd like to take a look.'

Then the students gathered around the master curiously, without a sound, as though they did not want to disturb the new atmosphere. Monsieur Seurel's half-curly, half-bald head bent over the treasures, while the pale young man gave the necessary explanations with a calm but triumphant air. Meaulnes, silent and abandoned on his bench, opened his rough-copy book, and, frowning, buried himself in a difficult problem.

We were still absorbed by the objects when it came time for morning break. Dictation remained unfinished and disorder reigned in the classroom. To be honest, we spent the entire morning at play.

When we burst out into the gloomy, muddy playground at half past ten, it was easy to see that a new leader was in charge. Of all the games the gypsy introduced us to, I only remember the most bloody. It was a sort of tournament where the older students were horses ridden by younger boys perched on their shoulders. Divided into two groups, one at either end of the schoolyard, the 'horses' swooped towards the centre, each trying to bring down his opponent with the force of impact. Meanwhile, the riders, using scarves as lassos or holding out their arms like lances, attempted to dislodge their rivals. Some dodged a collision but, losing their balance, landed spreadeagled in the mud, the rider rolling under his mount. Others, half dislodged, were caught by 'the horse', climbed back on to his shoulders, and returned to the struggle. Mounted on Delage, who had excessively long limbs, red hair, and jug ears, the slender knight of the bandaged head exhorted the rival troops and deftly steered his mount, all the while hooting with laughter.

Augustin, standing on the classroom threshold, watched these games with ill humour at first. I stood next to him, wavering.

'Cunning,' he said through clenched teeth, hands plunged deep in his pockets. 'Coming here this morning was the only way for him to avoid suspicion. And Monsieur Seurel has fallen for it!'

Meaulnes stayed there a long while, his shaved head catching the wind, muttering that this idiot would soon destroy all these troops whom he, Meaulnes, had so recently led. Peacekeeper that I was, I went along with him.

In the absence of the schoolmaster, the battle continued in all corners of the yard. The smallest boys ended up climbing on each other. They ran and tumbled over before they even made contact with their adversaries. Soon no one was left standing in the middle of the schoolyard except for a relentless, swirling group from which the white bandage of the new chief would appear from time to time.

Meaulnes could no longer hold back. He lowered his head, placed his hands on his thighs, and yelled, 'Let's go, François!'

Surprised by this sudden decision, I nonetheless jumped onto his shoulders without hesitating, and in an instant we were in the middle of the fray, overcoming most of the combatants, who fled, screaming,

'Here comes Meaulnes! Here comes Meaulnes the Magnificent!'

In the middle of those who remained standing, Meaulnes spun around, ordering me to reach out and grab them the way he had done the night before.

Intoxicated by the fight and confident of triumph, I snatched at boys who struggled as they passed, swaying for a moment on the shoulders of the 'horses,' and then falling in the mud. In no time, the only ones still standing were the newcomer and his mount, Delage. But Delage, not anxious to engage in a struggle with Augustin, straightened up and, with a violent shrug, forced the white knight to dismount.

With his hand on his steed's shoulder, the way a captain holds his horse by the bridle, the knight looked at Meaulnes, surprised into admiration.

'Well done!' he said.

Just then the bell rang, scattering the schoolboys who had gathered around us hoping for more excitement. Meaulnes, angry at not having the chance to hurl his enemy to the ground, turned his back, and said bad-temperedly, 'Until next time.'

Classes carried on until midday in a carnival atmosphere, and included a series of amusing interludes and conversations in which the gypsy was the focus.

He explained that he and his companion had been held up by the cold and could not mount their evening shows in the square because no one would come. So they had decided that he would go to school to occupy himself during the day, while his friend looked after the exotic birds and the trained goat. Then he told stories about their travels in the surrounding countryside, about the downpour that streamed on to them through the corroded zinc of the caravan's roof, and about climbing down the sides of the caravan and pushing on the wheel to get them out of the mud. The boys in the back row left their bench and came closer to listen. Those less romantically inclined profited from the moment to warm themselves around the stove. Soon, however, curiosity got the better of them and they too leaned towards the talkative bunch, straining their ears, but keeping one hand on the lid of the stove to save their place.

'What do you live on?' asked Monsieur Seurel, who was following all this and asking lots of questions with rather childlike curiosity for a schoolmaster.

The young man hesitated for a moment, as if he had never considered this little detail.

'What we earned in the autumn, I think,' he replied. 'Ganache keeps the accounts.'

No one asked who Ganache was. But I suspected he was the big lout who, the previous evening, had so treacherously attacked Meaulnes from behind and knocked him to the ground.

CHAPTER IV

BACK TO THE TOPIC OF THE MYSTERIOUS DOMAIN

THE afternoon brought the same amusement and the same disorder and deception during our lessons. The stranger produced other precious objects: shells, games, songs, and even a little monkey which clawed silently at the interior of his satchel. Monsieur Seurel kept interrupting himself to examine what this crafty boy had just pulled out of his bag. Four o'clock came, and Meaulnes was the only one who had finished his problems.

Everyone left slowly. It seemed as though there was no longer the hard line between lessons and recreation that makes the scholar's life as simple and regulated as the succession of night and day. We even forgot to inform Monsieur Seurel at ten to four which two students would stay behind and sweep the classroom; an unfailing ritual that drew attention to the end of the school day and speeded things up.

By chance it was Meaulnes's turn. And all morning I kept warning the stranger, whenever I chatted with him, that he would be the second sweeper, as this was expected of all new students on their first day. Meaulnes came back to the classroom as soon as he had fetched a piece of bread for his afternoon snack. But the stranger kept us waiting a long time and then came running in, just as night was beginning to fall.

'Stay here,' Meaulnes had directed me, 'and when I grab him, take back the map he stole from me.'

So I sat down at a little table near the window, reading by the last light of day, and watched them moving the school benches around in silence – Meaulnes, tall, taciturn, stern-faced, in his black smock with three buttons down the back and his tightly buckled belt; the other boy, delicate, nervous, his head bandaged like a wounded man's. He wore a shabby overcoat with rips I had not noticed during the day. Filled with savage fervour, he heaved the tables around fanatically, a little smile twitching his lips. It was as though he were playing a peculiar game for which we did not know the rules.

Then they arrived at the darkest corner of the room, and were about to move the last table.

With a mere flick of the wrist, Meaulnes could easily have knocked his adversary down in this corner without anyone outside seeing or hearing them through the windows. I did not understand why he let such an opportunity go. As soon as the other boy neared the door, he could flee at any moment on the pretext of having finished the job, and we would never see him again. The map and all the information that Meaulnes had spent so much time amassing, verifying, and assembling would be gone.

Each second I expected a sign from my comrade, a movement which would announce the beginning of the assault. But Meaulnes did not make his move. Occasionally he looked fixedly at the stranger's bandage, which in the half-light of evening appeared to have a large, dark stain.

They shifted the last table and swept the corner without anything else happening. But at the moment when they both returned to the front of the classroom to give a final sweep to the threshold, Meaulnes lowered his head and, without looking at our enemy, said quietly, 'Your bandage is red with blood and your clothes are torn.'

The stranger glanced at him, not surprised but profoundly moved by what Meaulnes had said to him.

'They wanted to snatch your map from me just now, in the square,' he replied. 'When they knew I had to come back here to sweep the classroom, they figured out that I would make peace with you, and they rebelled against me. But I hung on to it all the same,' he added proudly, handing the precious folded paper to Meaulnes.

My companion turned slowly towards me, 'Do you hear this? He has just fought and been wounded for us, while we were setting a trap for him!'

Addressing the stranger in a much warmer voice, Meaulnes announced, 'You are a true friend!' and held out his hand.

The stranger seized it, saying nothing for a moment, emotion rendering him speechless. But his curiosity soon overcame him and he continued, 'So you set a trap for me! How amusing. I guessed you would, and told myself that you would be stunned when, having taken back the map from me, you discovered that I had completed it.'

'Completed it?'

'Wait! Not entirely.'

Shedding his light-hearted tone and coming close to us, he added gravely and slowly, 'Meaulnes, it's time I told you. I, too, have been where you went. I was present at those fantastic celebrations. When the boys from here told me about your strange adventure, I deduced that it had to do with the old, lost domain. To confirm this, I stole your map. But, like you, I don't know the name of the manor and I wouldn't know how to return there because I don't know the direct route from here to there.'

With what joy, curiosity, and growing friendship we closed in on him! Meaulnes blurted out questions. By putting pressure on our new friend, we felt we could make him tell us what he claimed not to know.

'You will see. You will see,' the young man replied, slightly irritably. 'I have added some information to the map. That's all I could do.'

Then, noticing our wild enthusiasm, he said sadly but proudly: 'I must warn you. I am not like other boys. Three months ago I wanted to put a bullet through my head, and that explains the bandage over my forehead and why I look like a recruit after the Battle of the Seine in 1870.'

'And this evening while you were fighting, the wound opened up again?' asked Meaulnes sympathetically.

Without answering, the other boy continued in deliberate tones.

'I wanted to die. And since I did not succeed, I shall continue to live only for fun, like a child, like a vagabond. I have abandoned everything. I no longer have a father, a sister, a house, or love. Nothing but friends.'

'Those friends have already betrayed you,' I said.

'Yes,' he replied with animation. 'It's all Delouche's fault. He's the one who guessed I was going join forces with you. He demoralised the troops I had so well in hand. You saw how the attack was conducted yesterday evening, how well it went. I have never organised anything as successful since I was a child.'

He paused in thought for a moment and then added, as if to disabuse us of any illusions, 'If I have come over to your side this evening, it is because – and I realised it this morning – more pleasure can be had with you than with that band of others. Delouche especially annoys me. How stupid he is to pretend to be a grown man at seventeen. Nothing disgusts me more than pretension. Do you think we could grab him again?'

'Certainly. Do you plan to stay with us a while?'

'I don't know. I'd like to very much. I am terribly alone, with only Ganache for company.'

All his excitement, all his cheerfulness suddenly evaporated. In an instant he was plunged back into the same kind of despair which had led him to the idea of suicide.

'Be my friends,' he said suddenly. 'Look, I know your secret and I have defended it wholeheartedly. I can put you back on track.' Then he added solemnly, 'Be my friends to guard against the day when I will once again be two inches away from hell. Promise me to respond when I call you – when I call you like this,' and he gave a strange little cry: 'Hou-ou. You, Meaulnes, swear first.'

We swore because, children that we were, such solemnity fascinated us.

'In return,' he said, 'here's what I can offer you: the location of the house in Paris where the young lady of the manor usually spends Easter and Pentecost, the month of June, and part of the winter.'

At that moment, a voice we did not recognise cried out several times from the darkness near the main entrance.

We guessed it was Ganache, who did not dare cross the school-yard. Urgently, anxiously, sometimes loudly, sometimes softly came the call, 'Hou-ou. Hou-ou.'

'Tell us. Tell us quickly,' cried Meaulnes to our new friend, who shivered and gathered his coat around him as he prepared to leave.

He quickly whispered an address in Paris, which we repeated under our breath. Then he ran into the shadow to join his companion at the gate, leaving us in a state of complete turmoil.

CHAPTER V

THE MAN IN ESPADRILLES

AT three o'clock in the morning, the widow Delouche, the innkeeper who lived in the middle of the village, rose from her bed to light the fire. Dumas, her brother-in-law, who lived with her, was due to leave at four. The poor woman, whose right hand was shrivelled up from an old burn, hurried into the cold, dark kitchen to prepare coffee. She drew an old shawl over her nightdress, and then, holding a lighted candle in her good hand and sheltering it with the bad, she crossed the courtyard, all cluttered with soap boxes and empty bottles. She made for the woodshed, which also served as a henhouse, to fetch some twigs in her apron. Scarcely had she pushed the door open when a figure rose out of the blackness and killed the flame with a violent, whistling swipe of his cap. In the same blow, he knocked the poor woman down and then took to his heels. The terrified chickens set up a diabolical cackling.

Once she was back on her feet, Madame Delouche realised that the man had carried off a dozen of her best hens in his sack.

Hearing his sister-in-law's shouts, Dumas rushed outside. Accustomed to the behaviour of poachers and petty thieves, he quickly concluded that the scoundrel must have gained entry to the little courtyard with a stolen key and then fled by the same route, leaving the door open. He immediately lit a carriage lamp, holding it up in one hand and his loaded pistol in the other, and tried to follow the thief's scarcely definable tracks; the man must have been wearing espadrilles. The tracks led to the station road and then petered out in front of a gate to a meadow. Forced to abandon his search, he lifted his head, waited – and heard in the distance, on the same road, the sound of a carriage fleeing at full gallop.

Jasmin Delouche, the widow's son, got up and went outside in his slippers to see what was going on, hurriedly throwing a cape over his shoulders as he set off. Everything in the village was deeply asleep, in the profound silence that precedes the first glimmers of daylight. Like his uncle, all he heard when he arrived at Four-Roads was the sound of a carriage with its horse galloping away at the double, far off on Riandes hill. The spiteful, boastful boy then said to himself – something he repeated to us afterwards in the vulgar, guttural speech of the outskirts of Montluçan – 'That lot went towards the station, but I bet I can flush out more of them at the other end of town.'

He turned around and went back to the church through the still-silent night.

On the square, a light was shining in the caravan. Perhaps some-one was ill. He was just about to approach and ask, when a shadow – a shadow wearing espadrilles – materialised noiselessly from Little-Corners and ran swiftly towards the steps of the caravan without glancing right or left.

Recognising Ganache, Jasmin suddenly emerged into the light and demanded, 'So, what's going on?'

Ganache stopped in his tracks, haggard, dishevelled, toothless, terrified, and breathless. Then he replied jerkily, 'My companion is sick. He was in a fight yesterday. His wound opened up again. I went to find a nursing sister.'

Indeed, as Jasmin Delouche, burning with curiosity, headed back home to bed, he did encounter a nun, a nursing sister, hurrying along towards the centre of town.

In the morning, several inhabitants of Sainte-Agathe, who had all passed a sleepless night, appeared on their doorsteps with bags under their eyes. They were outraged, and their indignant assertions and speculations spread through the town like wildfire.

Around two o'clock in the morning, the two women at

Giraudat's place heard a cart stop and someone sling soft bundles into it. They were alone, and dared not stir until daybreak. Then they went out into the yard and realised that the bundles in question contained their rabbits and chickens. Millie, during our first break, found several half-burned matches in front of the laundry house. We concluded that the robbers had been misinformed about our building and had been unable to break in. Perreux, Boujardon, and Clément thought at first that the thieves had stolen their pigs, but these animals were found again during the morning, busy uprooting lettuces in various gardens; the whole pack had profited from open gates for a night-time promenade. Almost everyone had lost chickens but nothing else. Madame Pignot, the baker, who did not raise animals herself, moaned all day long that someone had stolen her carpet beater and a pound of washing blue, but this was never proved nor entered into the official report.

Panic, fear, and gossip circulated all morning. In class, Jasmin recounted the night's adventure.

'Oh, they're evil,' he told us. 'If my uncle had run into them, he would have gunned them down like rabbits. It's just as well he didn't see Ganache because he would have shot him too. He says they're all the same breed, and Dessaigne says so too.'

However, no one even considered bothering our new friends. It was not until the following evening that Jasmin remarked to his uncle that Ganache, like the thief, wore espadrilles. They agreed it was worth mentioning this to the authorities, and decided to go in secret, at the earliest opportunity, to alert the chief of police.

In the days that followed, we saw no sign of the injured gypsy.

Every evening, we roamed around the church square in the hope of seeing his lamp shining behind the red curtains of the caravan. Full of anxiety and excitement, we hung around without daring to approach the humble shack on wheels, which seemed to us to represent both the mysterious passage and antechamber to the domain whose path we had lost.

CHAPTER VI

A QUARREL IN THE WINGS

SO many trials and tribulations had prevented us from noticing that March had arrived and the wind had died down. But on the third day after this last adventure, when I went out into the schoolyard, I suddenly realised it was spring. A delicious breeze flowed over the top of the wall like warm water, and silent rain during the night had moistened the peony leaves; the raked earth in the garden smelled good enough to eat, and I heard a bird trying out his repertoire in the tree next to the window.

During our first break, Meaulnes immediately suggested that we investigate straight away the itinerary specified by our gypsy-schoolmate. With great difficulty I persuaded him to wait until we had seen our friend again, and the weather was truly favourable, and all the plum trees in Sainte-Agathe were in flower. We held our conversation leaning against the low wall of the little alley, bare-headed, with our hands in our pockets, the wind sometimes making us shiver and other times stirring up a sort of atavistic fervour with warm gusts. Ah, brother, companion, fellow traveller, how easily we were both persuaded that happiness was at hand, and all we had to do was to set off in its direction!

At half past twelve, during lunch, we heard a roll of drums on Four-Roads Square. In the blink of an eye, we were at the gate, our napkins still in our hands. It was Ganache, announcing a grand spectacle in the church square at eight o'clock that evening, weather permitting. In any case, a tent would be raised as protection against rain. He further announced a long list of attractions that the wind

104

carried away, but we could vaguely distinguish the words 'pantomimes, songs, fantasies on horseback', all accompanied by drum rolls.

During dinner that evening, the bass drum announcing the performance thundered under our windows and made the panes rattle. Soon afterwards, people from the outskirts of town passed by in a buzz of conversation, heading for the church square. And there we were, Meaulnes and I, forced to stay at the table, jiggling with impatience.

At last, towards nine o'clock, we heard the scraping of feet and stifled laughter at the gate. Our teachers had come to fetch us. In complete darkness, we set off in a group towards the performance site. From a distance we could see the church wall, lit as though by a huge fire. Two huge oil lamps hung in front of the stands, swinging in the wind.

Inside the makeshift tent, the tiers were organised the way they are in a circus tent. Monsieur Seurel, the teachers, Meaulnes and I seated ourselves on the lowest tier. I remember this space, which actually must have been quite small, as though it were a real circus enclosure, with huge layers of shadow where Madame Pignot (the baker), and Fernande (the grocer), village girls, blacksmith's helpers, urchins, peasants, and all manner of others were seated, row upon row.

The performance was more than half over. We could see a little performing goat on the stage, placing her feet very carefully on four glasses, then on two, then on just one. Ganache controlled her with gentle taps of his stick, looking towards us with an anxious air, his mouth open, his eyes dead.

On a stool near two more oil lamps, at the point where the stage met the caravan, sat the ringmaster – whom we recognised as our friend by his bandaged head – wearing a handsome black costume.

Scarcely had we sat down when a gaily harnessed pony galloped on to the stage, and the young man with the bandage made it circle around several times. Each time he required it to indicate the most amiable or brave person in the community, it stopped in front of one of our group, but if it was a matter of revealing who lied the most, was the greediest or the most amorous, it stopped directly before Madame Pignot. The people surrounding her started laughing, shouting, and honking – like a flock of geese pursued by a spaniel.

At the intermission, the ringmaster came to chat with Monsieur Seurel, who could not have more proud had he been talking to Talma or Léotard. And we – well, we listened raptly to everything he said: about his wound – closed up again; about this performance – prepared during the long days of winter; about their departure – which would not happen before the end of the month because they planned to give several different performances before then.

The spectacle would finish with a splendid mime show.

Towards the end of the interval, our friend left us. In order to get back to the caravan, he had to cut through a crowd that had invaded the ring, in the middle of which we suddenly noticed Jasmin Delouche. The women and girls stepped aside to let the ringmaster through. The black costume, the strange, brave bearing of an injured man, had captivated them all. As for Jasmin, he appeared to have just returned from a journey and was talking in a low, animated voice to Madame Pignot, but it was clear that someone wearing a sailor's rope belt, wide collar and bell bottoms would have been more to her taste. Jasmin stood with his thumbs in the lapels of his waistcoat, both smug and awkward. When the gypsy paused as he passed them, Delouche said something spiteful very loudly to Madame Pignot, something I could not hear but which was certainly an insult, a provocative remark about our new friend. It must have been a significant and unexpected threat because the young man could not help turning back and staring at Delouche. Jasmin, determined not to lose face, sniggered and nudged his neighbours to make certain they were on his side. All this happened in a few seconds, and without a doubt I was the only one on my bench to notice it.

The ringmaster rejoined his companion behind the curtain hiding the entrance to the caravan. Everyone returned to their seats on the tiers, believing that that the second half of the performance was about to begin and silence descended. But as the final whispered conversations died away, a noisy dispute broke out from behind the curtain. We could barely hear the words, although the voices of the gypsy and his companion were recognisable, the first explaining and justifying, the second reprimanding with a mixture of indignation and sadness.

'You idiot!' exclaimed the second. 'Why didn't you tell me?'

We couldn't hear what followed, even though we were all ears. Suddenly everything went silent, and then the altercation began again, very softly.

The crowd at the top of the tiers began to stamp their feet and call out:

'Lights! Curtain!'

CHAPTER VII

THE GYPSY REMOVES HIS BANDAGE

AT last, with a sparkle of sequins, a head eased slowly between the curtains, its face furrowed by lines in a contradiction of expressions, wide-eyed one moment with gaiety and the next with distress. Then the body of a tall clown emerged in three badly articulated parts, his hands tangled up in sleeves so long that they swept the ground. Hunched over as though he had colic, he walked cautiously and fearfully on tiptoe.

Today I can no longer reconstruct the plot of his mime. I only remember that almost as soon as he arrived in the ring, after trying desperately to stay on his feet, he fell. He had trouble getting up. He fell again. And again. He couldn't stop falling. He got tangled up with four chairs, and fell again, pulling over an enormous table someone had left on the stage. He ended up in the audience, sprawled at some spectators' feet. Two assistants, solicited with difficulty from the public, pulled him back on stage and set him upright with enormous effort. Each time he fell, he gave a different little cry, an unbearable little cry in which distress and satisfaction were equally mixed. Finally, he climbed on top of a pile of chairs, and fell slowly from its height with a strident, miserable, triumphant hoot that lasted as long as the fall, and was accompanied by shrieks of terror from the women in the audience.

During the second part of 'the poor falling pierrot's' pantomime, I saw him produce a little bran-stuffed doll from the depths of one of his sleeves. He mimed an entire tragicomedy with her, at the end of which he made her spew all the bran in her stomach out through her mouth. Then with pitiful little whimpers he filled her up with porridge, and when all the spectators were rapt with attention, open-mouthed, their eyes fixed on the slimy toy, he suddenly seized her by an arm and hurled her across the audience, as hard as he could, at Jasmin Delouche. She barely grazed his ear before going Splat! on Madame Pignot's chest, just below her chin. Madame Pignot gave a loud cry and fell back hard, taking with her all her neighbours, which broke the bench, and the widow Delouche, Fernande, and twenty others also fell backwards, legs in air, to the accompaniment of laughter and applause. The tall clown, flat on the ground, slowly lifted himself up and took his leave, saying:

'Ladies and gentlemen, we have been honoured by your presence.'

At that very moment, in the middle of this immense commotion, Meaulnes, who had been silent since the beginning of the mime show, completely absorbed by it, rose up suddenly, seized me by the arm and, no longer able to hold back, cried out to me:

'Look at the gypsy! Look over there! I recognise him at last.'

Even before I looked, I had been coming to the same conclusion. Standing near a lamp at the entry to the caravan, the young man undid his bandage and threw a cape over his shoulders. We could see his fine, clean-shaven, aquiline face in the smoky light, the same face Meaulnes had seen by candlelight at the lost estate. Pale, his lips half-open, he began hurriedly leafing through a little red album which looked like a pocket atlas. Except for the scar cutting across his temple and disappearing into his mass of hair, he exactly met Meaulnes's description of the fiancé from the mysterious estate.

He had clearly taken off his bandage so that we should recognise him. But just as Meaulnes made a move and called out to him, he went back into the caravan, giving us a knowing look and his usual sad smile.

'And the other one,' said Meaulnes frantically, 'why didn't I recognise him either? He's the pierrot from the celebrations at the estate!'

Meaulnes clambered down the tiers towards him, but Ganache had already removed all access to the stage, and one by one he was extinguishing the four oil lamps that illuminated the arena. Writhing with impatience, we were obliged to follow the crowd in the dark, in slow lines channelled between the rows of seats, virtually at a standstill.

The moment he made it outside, Meaulnes rushed towards the caravan, leaped on to the step, and rapped at the door. It was firmly closed. In that curtained cabin, just as in the pony's stall, the goat's byre, and the wild birds' cage, the occupants had retired for the night and were settling down to sleep.

CHAPTER VIII

POLICE!

WE had to join up with a group of men and women winding along dark streets towards the school. But we understood everything now. The huge, white silhouette, which Meaulnes had seen flitting in and out of the trees on the last evening of celebrations at the domain, was Ganache. He had taken charge of the desperate fiancé and escaped with him in tow. Frantz de Galais had completely accepted Ganache's peripatetic existence, with its risks, games, and adventures. It made him feel as though he were starting childhood all over again.

Until then, Frantz de Galais hid his identity from us, pretending not to know the way back to the estate, and worried no doubt about being forced to return to his parents. But why, on that particular evening, had he suddenly revealed himself to us, allowing us to guess the whole truth?

Meaulnes conjured up all kinds of fantastical plans as the crowd of spectators drifted slowly across the town. He decided he would go and find Franz the very next morning, which happened to be a Thursday. Together, they would set out for the domain. What a trip it would be on that muddy road! Franz would explain what had happened, everything would fall into place, and the marvellous adventure would start up all over again at the point where it had been interrupted.

As for me, I walked through the darkness, my heart pounding with inexpressible joy. Everything contributed to this joy, from the subtle feeling of pleasure caused by the anticipation of Thursday, to the thrill of the discovery we had just made, to astonishment at the great stroke of fortune that had befallen us. I remember suddenly feeling so generous that I even approached the ugliest of the notary's daughters – the torture of offering her my arm had occasionally been imposed on me – and spontaneously took her hand.

All this anticipation is now a bitter memory.

The next day, at eight o'clock, Meaulnes and I set off for the church square sporting our new caps, with our shoes well shined and belt buckles polished. Meaulnes who had up to then managed to suppress a laugh when he looked at me, gave a shout, and rushed into the square. It was empty! Where stalls and carriages had stood, nothing but a broken pot and some rags remained. The vagabonds had disappeared.

A chill gust of wind made us shiver. With each step, we seemed in danger of tripping over the uneven surface in the square. Meaulnes, in a panic, set off twice, first in the direction of Vieux-Nançay, and the second time towards Saint Loup-des-Bois. He kept peering into the distance with his hand shading his eyes, trying to catch a glimpse of our friends. We had no idea which way to go because at least ten different cart tracks were mixed up together in the square and then petered out on the hard roads. All we could do was stand there uselessly.

As we made our way home through the village that early Thursday morning, four policemen on horseback, alerted by Delouche the previous evening, burst into the square at a gallop and spread out to block all the exits, like dragoons reconnoitring a village. But they were too late. Ganache, the notorious chicken thief, had fled with his companion. The police found no one, not him, nor even those who loaded the carts with the chickens whose necks he had wrung.

Alerted by Jasmin's careless word, Franz must have suddenly understood what activity supported him and his companion when funds ran short in the caravan cashbox. Ashamed and furious, he quickly plotted out a route and took to the fields before the arrival of the police. No longer fearing an attempt to take him back to his father's estate, he decided to reveal himself to us without his bandage before disappearing.

One issue remained obscure: how could Ganache have been ransacking a farmyard at the same time as he was summoning a nurse for his friend? But wasn't that the poor devil's life story? Thief and vagabond on one hand, kindly saviour on the other.

CHAPTER IX

LOOKING FOR THE LOST PATH

WE returned home through the most radiant spring morning I can remember, just as the sun was dissipating a light morning mist and housewives on their doorsteps were chatting or shaking out their rugs.

The senior students were all due to arrive at eight o'clock to study during the morning, some for the school-leaving certificate and others for the university entrance examinations. When we arrived – Meaulnes, too full of disappointment and agitation to stay still, and I, completely demoralised – the school was empty. A sunbeam showed up the dust on a worm-eaten bench and on the flaking varnish of a globe.

How could we stay there, hidden behind our books, mulling over our disappointment, when everything outside called us? Birds chased each other in the branches near the windows, and our fellow students had fled to the meadows and woods. But above all, we burned with feverish desire to investigate the sections of the route the gypsy had verified – the last resource in our almost empty bag, the one last key to turn. But we didn't know where to start. Meaulnes marched to and fro, going up to the windows, looking out into the garden, then coming back and looking towards the town, as if he were waiting for someone unlikely to arrive.

'I think . . .' he said at last, 'I think it is not as far as we imagine. Frantz deleted one whole part of the trail I had marked on the map, and perhaps this means the mare made a long, useless detour while I slept.'

I was perched on the corner of a large table, discouraged and disheartened, my head down, one foot on the ground, the other dangling.

'Even so,' I said, 'your journey back here lasted all night.'

'We left at midnight,' he snapped back. 'I was deposited at four o'clock in the morning, approximately six kilometres to the west of Sainte-Agathe, but I had left by the Rue de la Gare to the east. We must therefore subtract six kilometres between Sainte-Agathe and the lost domain. I am now convinced that when you leave the town forest, you are no more than two leagues from what we're looking for.'

'But it is precisely those two leagues that are missing from your map.'

'Precisely! And the way out of the forest is a league and a half from here, but a good walker could easily do that in a morning.'

Just then, Moucheboeuf arrived. He had an irritating way of pretending to be a diligent student, not by working harder than others, but by drawing attention to himself in a situation like this.

'I knew it,' he said triumphantly. 'I knew I would find the two of you alone here. Everyone else has left for the town forest, with Jasmin Delouche at the head – he knows where the birds' nests are.'

Then, pretending to be on our side, he began recounting how they had made fun of the school, of Monsieur Seurel, and of us while they planned their expedition.

'If they are in the forest, I will probably see them as I pass through, because I'm off too,' said Meaulnes. 'I will be back around half past twelve.'

Moucheboeuf was dumbfounded.

'Aren't you coming?' Augustin asked me, stopping for a moment on the threshold of the open door. Into the room blew a gust of sun-warmed air, accompanied by cries, calls, chirps, and other more distant sounds, like a bucket hitting the coping of a well and the cracking of a whip.

'No,' I said, though sorely tempted. 'I can't because of Monsieur Seurel. But go on – and hurry back and tell me about it.'

He made a vague gesture and left quickly, full of hope.

When Monsieur Seurel arrived at about ten o'clock, he had removed his alpaca jacket and replaced it with a fisherman's coat with vast buttoned pockets, a straw hat, and short, glossy gaiters that kept the bottom of his trousers in place. I am sure he was surprised to find anyone here at all, and certainly did not need Mouchebouef to repeat three times what the boys had said: 'If he needs us so much, let him come and find us!'

'Tidy up, grab your caps, and we will flush them out. Can you walk that far, François?'

I agreed I could, and we set off.

We put Moucheboeuf in the lead, to serve as Monsieur Seurel's decoy. Knowing the location of the particular cluster of trees where the nest-robbers might be found, he called out loudly from time to time:

'Yoo-hoo! Giraudat! Delouche! Where are you? Have you found anything?'

To my delight, I was given the task of patrolling the eastern boundary of the woods in case the runaways were looking for an escape by that route. I was pleased because, on the map the gypsy had corrected that Meaulnes and I studied time and time again, there appeared to be a narrow, dirt track which left from this side of the woods in the direction of the estate. If only I could find it! I managed to persuade myself that, before noon, I would find myself on the path that led to the lost manor house.

What a wonderful outing! As soon as we passed Les Glacis and made a detour around the windmill, I left my two companions, Monsieur Seurel, who looked as though he were setting off for war (and I know for certain that he had put an old pistol in his pocket) and the turncoat Moucheboeuf. Taking a shortcut, I soon arrived alone at the edge of the forest, venturing across country for the first time in my life, like a patrol that has lost its corporal.

Here I am, I imagine, close to the mysterious happiness that Meaulnes had glimpsed. I have the whole morning to explore the edge of the forest, the coolest and most secret place in the area, while my big friend is already launched on his journey of discovery. The path looks like an old river bed. I pass under the low branches of trees whose name I don't know but are probably alders. A little while ago, I climbed over a stile at the end of the footpath, to find myself on a wide, grassy track flowing like a stream under the leaves, brushing against clumps of nettles and crushing tall valerian plants.

Now and then I feel sand underfoot. I hear a bird singing – I imagine it is a nightingale, but no doubt I am wrong since nightingales only sing at night. This bird obstinately repeats its morning song again and again, trilling from the shade a delightful invitation to wander among the alders. Invisible, it persists in following me through the foliage.

For the first time, I am alone, me, myself, François, on the path to adventure. I am not searching for shells under the direction of Monsieur Seurel, nor for orchids that the school master himself can not identify, nor even, as we often did in old Martin's field, for the deep but dried-out spring, covered by wire mesh and hidden under such a tangle of weeds that each time it takes longer to find.

I am searching for something still more mysterious: that pathway mentioned in books, that ancient blocked way, the one to which the exhausted prince can find no entrance. It reveals itself at a lost moment in the morning when time has ceased to make sense. Is it eleven o'clock? Twelve? Suddenly, as I push aside some branches in the dense foliage, hesitating, my hands reaching out at eye level, I see a long, dark avenue with a tiny circle of light at the end.

Full of hope and exhilaration, I burst out precipitately into a sort of clearing, which turns out to be an ordinary meadow. Without realising it, I have arrived at the limit of the town forest, which I have always imagined to be infinitely further away. And here on my right, between stacks of wood, everything buzzing in the shade, is the forester's house. Two pairs of socks are drying on the windowsill.

Years ago, when we arrived at the entrance to the forest, we always said, pointing to a fleck of light at the end of the long dark avenue, 'Over there is Baladier the forester's house.' We had never ventured as far as it, but had heard it said of others, as though it were an extraordinary feat, 'He has been as far as the forester's house.'

This time I had gone as far as Baladier's house, but I had found nothing.

My poor weak leg began to tire, and the heat, which I hadn't noticed until then, became oppressive. I was growing frightened about finding the way back all by myself when I suddenly heard Monsieur Seurel's decoy, Moucheboeuf, nearby, and then other voices calling me.

It was six big lads – Giraudat, Auberger, Delage and three others – only one of whom, the traitor Moucheboeuf, looked pleased with himself. He had cornered some boys up a cherry tree in the middle of a clearing and found others in the act of flushing woodpeckers from their nests. Giraudat, that idiot with swollen eyes and filthy overalls, had some nestlings hidden in a pouch between his shirt and skin. Delouche and little Coffin had already fled at Monsieur Seurel's approach, but the rest of the gang at first responded to Moucheboeuf with insults, calling him 'Mouchevache', and the word echoed through the woods. He, vexed and mistakenly believing himself in control of the situation, threatened:

'You'd better come down, you know! Monsieur Seurel is here!'

Suddenly everything went silent. They had vanished into those woods they knew like the backs of their hands. There was no point in trying to catch up with them, and no one knew where Meaulnes had gone or heard his voice. We had to give up the search.

It was after noon by the time we started back to Sainte-Agathe, heads down, exhausted, and muddy. As we scraped the mud from our shoes on the dry road, after we had left the forest, the sun began to beat down on us hard. It was no longer a fresh and gleaming spring morning, and afternoon sounds started filling the air. In the distance, a cock crowed a desolate cry from one of the deserted farms along the road. We stopped for a moment at Les Glacis to chat with fieldhands who were just about to start work again after lunch. They leaned on the gate while Monsieur Seurel talked to them.

'What rascals these boys are! Take a look at Giraudat. He has put nestlings inside his shirt, and they've made their mess in there! Serves him right!'

It felt as though the fieldhands were also laughing at my predicament. They laughed and nodded their heads, but didn't quite condemn the boys they knew so well. And after Monsieur Seurel had gone back to the front of the line, they confided in us, saying:

'Another young fellow passed this way. You know, the tall fellow. He must have taken a lift on the coach from Les Granges, and got off here, covered in mud, his clothes in shreds. We told him we had seen you pass by this morning, but that you hadn't come back yet. And he continued on his way, walking slowly towards Sainte-Agathe.'

And indeed, Meaulnes was waiting for us, tired out, sitting on one of the bridge supports at Les Glacis. To Monsieur Seurel's questions, he replied that he, too, had taken part in the hunt for the truants. And to the question I asked him very quietly, he just said, shaking his head in discouragement, 'No. Nothing. Nothing like that.'

After lunch, he sat down at one of the big tables in the closed-up classroom, dark and empty in the middle of that radiant landscape and, head in arms, slept for a long time, a deep, sad sleep. Towards evening, he awoke and after a moment of reflection in which he appeared to make an important decision, he wrote a letter to his mother.

And that is all I remember of that dismal end to a day of failure.

CHAPTER X

THE LAUNDRY

WE counted too early on the arrival of spring.

On Monday, we were determined to finish our homework as soon as possible after the end of lessons, the way we did in full summer and, to take advantage of the light, we took two big tables out into the courtyard. But the sky clouded over immediately, a drop of rain fell on someone's exercise book, and we hurried back inside. Through the long windows of the large, dark room, we looked out at grey clouds scudding across the sky.

Meaulnes, watching like the rest of us, with one hand on the casement latch, could not help saying, as if he was bitter with regret, 'Huh! The clouds drifted past in a different fashion when I was travelling in the coach from Belle-Etoile.'

'On which road?' asked Jasmin.

Meaulnes did not reply.

To create a diversion, I announced, 'I'd like to travel in a coach like that, lashed by the rain, sheltered under a giant umbrella.'

'Reading all the way, as if you were in a house,' added someone.

'It was not raining and I did not want to read,' replied Meaulnes. 'I was intent on looking at the landscape.'

But when Giraudat in turn asked what landscape he was referring to, Meaulnes remained silent. Then Jasmin spoke up.

'I know. It's still that famous adventure of his.'

He said these words in a conspiratorial way, as though he were in on the secret. But it was a wasted effort, and his overture gained him nothing. As night was falling, everyone sped off into the freezing deluge with their smocks pulled up over their heads.

It rained until the following Thursday, a day which proved even more dismal than the previous Thursday. The entire landscape was wallowing in a sort of freezing fog. It felt just like the worst days of winter.

Millie, fooled by the previous week's beautiful sunshine, had insisted on doing the laundry, but it was impossible to drape the linen to dry on the hedges, or even on the washlines in the granary because the air was so humid and cold.

She discussed this with Monsieur Serel and he came up with the idea of hanging her laundry in the classroom since it was Thursday, and to make the stove white hot. To economise on fuel for the kitchen and living-room fires, our meals would be cooked on the stove and we would spend all day in the big classroom.

At first – how young I was! – this novelty felt like a celebration.

What a miserable celebration! The laundry soaked up all the warmth of the stove, and the room became incredibly cold. I was bored out of my mind. I went out into the schoolyard, where an interminable, winter drizzle was falling. Nevertheless, I found Meaulnes there, at nine o'clock in the morning. In silence, resting our heads on the main gate, we gazed through the bars towards Four-Roads at the high end of town. A funeral cortège wound slowly in from the countryside. The coffin, carried on an ox-cart, was then unloaded and placed on a slab at the foot of the big cross where, just a few days before, the butcher had seen the gypsy's sentinels! Where was he now, that young captain who had managed the assault so skilfully? The priest and the choir stood in their places in front of the coffin and their sad singing reached us from there. We knew that this event would be the only thing worth looking at during the entire day, a day which was dribbling along like sludgy water in a gutter.

'Now,' said Meaulnes suddenly, 'I am going to pack. I have news for you, Seurel. I wrote to my mother last Thursday asking her if I might finish my studies in Paris. I leave today.'

He kept looking towards the town, his hands gripping the railings at head height. It was useless to ask him if his mother, who was rich and pandered to his every whim, had agreed with his plan. It was also useless to demand why he was in such a hurry to go to Paris.

But I could see some regret in his face and fear at leaving dear Sainte-Agathe, the place from which he had first set out on his adventure. As for me, I was stricken by a mounting sense of desolation, which I had not felt at first.

'Easter is coming,' he explained with a sigh.

'You will write to me when you get there, won't you?' I asked.

'Of course. I promise you. Aren't you my friend and my brother?' He put his hand on my shoulder.

Little by little I understood that it was all over, and that he was determined to complete his education in Paris. Never again would I have my great friend beside me. The only hope of being reunited lay in the house in Paris where it might be possible to pick up the trail of the lost adventure. But if Meaulnes himself were so sad, what hope lay in store for me?

He informed my parents. Monsieur Seurel expressed astonishment, but soon understood the reasoning. Millie, the good housewife, was mainly upset by the thought that Meaulnes's mother would see our house festooned with wet laundry. Alas! All too soon we had packed his trunk, having dug his Sunday shoes out from under the staircase, found some linen in the armoire, and located his papers and schoolbooks – everything a young man of eighteen possessed in the world.

At noon, Madame Meaulnes arrived in her carriage. She ate at Café Daniel with Augustin, and took him away without any explanation as soon as the horse was fed and hitched up again. On the doorstep, we bade them farewell, and the carriage disappeared around the bend at Four-Roads.

Millie wiped her shoes outside the door and went back into the freezing dining room, putting everything back in its place. I found myself alone for the first time in many long months – facing an endless Thursday afternoon – with the impression that my adolescence had been carried away for ever in that old carriage.

CHAPTER XI

THE BETRAYAL

WHAT could I do?

The clouds lifted a bit and it looked as though the sun might come out.

A door slammed in the house. Then silence fell again. From time to time my father crossed the schoolyard to fill a bucket with charcoal to put in the stove. I caught a glimpse of white sheets hanging from lines in that dismal drying room. I hadn't the least desire to go back in there and get to grips with the upcoming, intensely competitive, university entrance examinations coming up at the end of the year, which should be my sole preoccupation from that moment on.

Now here's something strange: mixed in with this desolation I had a feeling of freedom. With the departure of Meaulnes, and with no satisfying outcome to the adventure, I felt liberated from anxiety, from the mysterious occupation that kept me from behaving like the rest of my fellows. With the departure of Meaulnes, I was no longer his companion-in-arms, hunting down trails with him. I was once again a village boy like the others. Life was easy. All I had to do was follow my instincts.

The youngest Roy passed by on the muddy road, twirling three conkers around on the end of a string, then letting them fly up in the air. They kept landing in the schoolyard, and my idleness was so great that I took pleasure in throwing them back over the wall each time.

Suddenly I saw him abandon his game and run towards a little waggon coming along the road from Vieille-Planche. It didn't even stop as he jumped quickly on to the back of it. It was Delouche's horse and cart, with Jasmin himself driving, and Fat Boy Boujardon was standing up beside him. They were coming from the meadow.

'Come with us, François!' cried Jasmin, who must have already heard that Meaulnes had left.

Well! Without telling anyone at home, I too climbed on to the jolting cart and stood up like the others, steadying myself by leaning against one of the uprights. We were on our way to Widow Delouche's.

She is not only an innkeeper but a grocer, and we are now in her shop. A ray of white sunshine slides across the low window on to tins of food and casks of vinegar. Fat Boujardon sits down on the windowsill and turns to us with a deep belly laugh as he stuffs himself with biscuits. The open box stands on top of a barrel within range of his hand, and he dips right in. Little Roy squeals with pleasure. We establish a sort of false intimacy, and I realise that Jasmin and Boujardon have become my new companions. The course of my life has suddenly changed. It seems as though Meaulnes left ages ago and that the great adventure is a sad old tale – but finished.

Little Roy has unearthed an open bottle of alcohol from under one of the counters. Delouche offers us each a taste, but there is only one glass, so we all drink from it. He serves me first, somewhat condescendingly, as though I were not used to the habits of peasants and hunters. This annoys me, and when someone begins to speak about Meaulnes, I decide to recover my nerve by showing them that I know his story and can tell them a bit about it. What harm can it do? All his adventures here are now things of the past.

Do I tell the story badly? It does not produce the effect I counted on. My companions, in their good village way, are unimpressed.

'So it was just a wedding. So what!' says Boujardon.

Delouche has seen a wedding at Préveranges which was even more peculiar.

The castle? No doubt, people around here know about it.

The young girl? Meaulnes will marry her after his military service.

'He should have talked to us and shown us his map instead of confiding in that gypsy.'

Mired in my lack of success, I want to take advantage of their curiosity. I decide to explain who the gypsy was, where he came from, and his strange destiny. Boujardon and Delouche want nothing to do with it.

'He's responsible for everything. He's the one who made Meaulnes so unsociable, Meaulnes who was so friendly at first. He's the one who organised all those stupid assaults and night attacks after recruiting us, a battalion of scholars.'

'You know,' says Jasmin, looking at Boujardon and giving his head a little shake, 'I certainly did the right thing when I reported him to the police. He's someone who did a lot of harm round here, and may do so again.'

I am almost convinced by their argument. Everything would have turned out differently had we not become so wrapped up in all the mystery and tragedy. It was because of Frantz that all was lost.

Suddenly, while I am thinking about this, we hear a noise in the front of the shop. Jasmin Delouche quickly hides the flask behind a barrel. Fat Boujardon tumbles down from the windowsill, lands on an empty, dusty bottle which rolls him along, and twice he just misses falling flat on his face. Choking with laughter, Little Roy shoves them from behind to make them leave more quickly.

I flee with them, without quite understanding why. We cross the courtyard and climb a ladder into a hayloft. I hear a woman's voice calling us good-for-nothings.

'I didn't think she'd be back so soon,' whispers Jasmin.

Only now do I realise that we came here for the sole purpose of stealing biscuits and booze. I am as deceived as the shipwrecked man who thinks he is talking to a man but suddenly realises he's talking to a monkey. I want more than anything to get away from this hayloft because I hate this kind of game. Besides, it's getting late.

They tell me how to leave by the back way: cross two gardens and go around the pond. Soaked to the skin and covered in mud, I find myself outside on the wet street, which reflects back the light shining from Café Daniel.

I am not proud of myself this evening. Here I am at Four-Roads. In spite of myself, I see again that stern but brotherly face looking at me from the bend in the road. A smile, a last wave of the hand – and the carriage disappears.

A cold wind flaps my smock. It is as cold as the wind that blew during all those miserable, marvellous winter months. Everything seems less easy now. In the big classroom, where they are waiting for me with dinner, sharp draughts dispense the meagre warmth of the stove. I shiver while I am reprimanded for my afternoon's vagrancy. I don't even have the comfort of regaining my old life by taking my usual seat at the table because the table has not been set this evening; everyone is eating off their knees wherever they can find a place in the dark classroom. I silently chew the pancake, meant to be a treat for having to spend this Thursday at school, but it has burnt circles on it because the stove-top was too hot.

In the evening, all alone in my room, I climb into bed quickly and try to smother the remorse I feel rising up through my sadness. I wake up twice in the middle of the night. The first time I think I hear the other bed creak, the way it did when Meaulnes suddenly turned over; the second time, I think I hear his footsteps at the far end of the attic, like the soft footsteps of a hunter on the lookout.

CHAPTER XII

THREE LETTERS FROM MEAULNES

IN my entire life, I only received three letters from Meaulnes. I still have them at home in my chest of drawers. Each time I re-read them, I experience the same sadness.

The first arrived two days after his departure.

My dear François,

As soon as I arrived in Paris today, I went to the house Frantz had spoken about. I saw nothing. No one was there. No one will ever be there. It is a little two-storey building. Mademoiselle de Galais's room must be on the first floor. The windows above are mostly hidden by trees, but if you walk along the pavement, you can easily see them. All the curtains are closed and it would be mad to hope that one day the face of Yvonne de Galais might appear between those drawn curtains.

The house is on a boulevard. Gentle rain was falling on the trees, which were already green. I kept hearing the clanging bells of passing tramcars.

For nearly two hours I walked up and down beneath the windows. I stopped in a nearby wine shop for a drink, so as not to be taken for a thief preparing to commit a crime. Then, without hope, I went back on watch.

Night came. Windows lit up almost everywhere – but not in that house. It is definite; no one is there even though Easter is approaching.

At the very moment I decided to leave, a girl, or young woman

– I don't know which – arrived and sat down on one of the wet benches. She was dressed in black with a little white ruff. She was still there when I left, motionless in spite of the evening's cold, waiting for what or whom I do not know. Paris is full of fools like me.

Augustin

Time passed. I waited in vain for a word from Augustin on Easter Monday and during all the days that followed – days of such calm after the immense fever of Easter that the only thing to look forward to was the advent of summer. June meant exams, incredible heat, and suffocating humidity hovering over the countryside with not even a breath of wind to clear it away. Night brought no relief and consequently no rest. It was during this unbearable June that I received the second letter from Meaulnes.

My dear friend,

This time, all hope is lost. I have known it since yesterday evening. The sorrow which I did not feel at first, now grows and grows.

I had been in the habit of going, each evening, to sit on the bench, watching, reflecting, and hoping in spite of everything.

Yesterday, after dinner, the night was dark and stuffy. People were chatting on the pavement under the trees. Apartments on the second and third floors were illuminated, their lights turning the dark foliage bright green. Here and there a window was wide open to let in the summer air; here and there I could see a lamp on a table, its light illuminating the whole room but barely keeping the hot, dark, June night at bay. Oh, if only Yvonne de Galais's window had been lit that way, I would have dared – I think – to climb the stairs, to knock, to enter.

The young woman, whom I have already mentioned, was there again, waiting like me. I thought she might know something about the occupants of the the house and so I questioned her.

'I believe,' she said, 'that in the past a young girl and her brother used to spend their holidays here. But I have since learned that the brother fled from his parents' castle, and no one has been able to find him. The young woman got married. That explains why the apartment is empty.'

I left. I had gone a mere ten steps when I stumbled on the pavement and nearly fell. Then late at night – this was last night – when at last the women and children in the courtyards had quietened down enough so that I could sleep, I began hearing taxi carriages rumbling along the street. They were merely plying their trade, but each time one passed, I started to anticipate the next in spite of myself, the bell, the horse's hoofs on the asphalt. And I kept hearing a refrain: empty town, lost love, interminable night, summer, fever . . .

Seurel, my friend, I am in utter despair.

Augustin

Even though they appeared to say something, these letters told me almost nothing. Meaulnes explained neither why he had been silent for so long nor what he planned to do. I had the impression that he was breaking off our friendship because his adventure was finished, just the way he was turning his back on his past. It didn't seem worth writing to him because he never replied, except to send a note of congratulations when I passed my school certificate. In September, I learned from a classmate that Meaulnes had come to spend the holidays at his mother's in La Ferté-d'Angillon, but that year, my uncle Florentin invited us to spend our vacation with him in Vieux-Nançay, and we were obliged to go there instead. And Meaulnes returned to Paris without my ever seeing him.

At the start of the new school year, towards the end of November to be exact, I applied myself with a sort of dismal fervour to preparing for the higher school certificate in the hope of being made a teacher the following year without having to go to the university in Bourges. It was just then that I received the third letter from Augustin:

I pass once more under this window, still stupidly waiting, without a shred of hope. At the end of these cold autumn Sundays, just as night falls, I cannot go home and shut myself in without first returning to this icy street. I am like the madwoman of Sainte-Agathe who goes out on to her doorstep and, with her hand above her eyes, looks towards the station to see if her dead son is returning to her.

Sitting on the bench, shivering, miserable, I find pleasure in imagining that someone will come and touch me gently on my arm. I will turn around. And she is there. 'I am a little late,' she says simply. All sorrow and madness dissipate. We enter our house. Her furs are covered in ice, her headscarf soaked. She brings into the house a taste of fog. While she draws closer to the fire, I notice the frost sparkling in her blonde hair, and her beautiful, gentle profile as she leans towards the flames.

But, alas, the white curtains remain closed behind the window. Anyway, even if the girl from the lost domain should open it, I would have nothing to say to her.

Our adventure is over. This winter is as dead as the tomb. Perhaps when we die, death will provide us with the key to what happened next and the conclusion of this ruined adventure.

Seurel, I once asked you to remember me. Now it would be better if you forgot me. It would be better to forget everything.

It is a new winter, as dead as the previous one had been embued with mysterious vitality. No gypsies prance around the church square; the schoolyard is deserted by four o'clock; the classroom, where I study alone, is empty of atmosphere. In February, for the first time this winter, it snows, burying, once and for all, the romantic adventures of the past year, blurring every path, effacing the final traces. I force myself to forget everything, just as Meaulnes requested in his letter.

PART III

CHAPTER I

SWIMMING

SMOKING cigarettes; putting sugar water on their hair to make it curl; kissing convent girls in the street; and, from behind the hedge, scoffing and crying out 'Here's to Conehead!' at a passing nun – all this was sport for the local pranksters. But strangely enough, when those boys reach twenty years of age, they often turn into reasonable young men. But the situation is graver when the prankster in question already looks old and jaded, when he spends his time seeking out salacious stories about local women, when he invents a thousand tales about Gilberte Poquelin just to make others laugh. But at last, even a hard case like this is not without hope.

This was how it went with Jasmin Delouche. He continued, I don't know why, to follow the syllabus for the higher certificate, but certainly without any intention of taking the exams. We all wished he would quit. In between classes, he was an apprentice to his uncle, a plasterer. And eventually, this same Jasmin Delouche, along with Boujardon and a gentle boy called Denis, the son of the deputy headmaster, were the only students I enjoyed spending time with – because they had been with me during the Meaulnes era.

Besides, Delouche sincerely wanted to be my friend. In fact, he who had been Meaulnes's greatest enemy, now wanted to imitate him and regretted not having been his lieutenant. Quicker-witted than Boujardon, he was well aware of everything extraordinary that Meaulnes had brought into our lives. I often heard him repeating, 'Meaulnes was right' or 'Ah, that's exactly what Meaulnes said.'

Jasmin was like a little old man who showed his superiority over us by flaunting his treasured possessions: a mongrel with long white hair, responding to the irritating name of Beaky Boo, who would retrieve stones thrown a long distance but had absolutely no other talent; an ancient, second-hand bicycle he sometimes let us ride in the evening after school, preferring, however, to impress girls with it; and last but not least, a blind, white donkey he could hitch up to any vehicle.

It was actually his uncle Dumas's donkey, but he lent it to Jasmin whenever we went swimming in the Cher during the summer. Jasmin's mother would give us a bottle of lemonade, which we put under the bench among our swimming costumes. Eight or ten older pupils, accompanied by Monsieur Seurel, set off on foot; others climbed onto the donkey cart, which we left at Grand'Fons when the path beside the Cher became too steep.

I have every reason to remember one particular occasion, down to the smallest details. Jasmin's donkey carried our swimsuits, our bags, the lemonade, and Monsieur Seurel while the rest of us followed on foot. It was August, and we had just taken our exams. Free from that worry, the whole, happy summer opened up before us, and there we were, at the beginning of a beautiful Thursday afternoon, walking along the road, singing our hearts out without knowing why.

As we strolled along, only one shadow fell on this innocent scene. This is what happened. Gilberte Poquelin was walking ahead of us. Her neat waist, calf-length skirt, high heels, and sweet, insolent air made us aware of a girl on the verge of womanhood. She left the road and took a roundabout path, probably to collect some milk. Little Coffin immediately suggested to Jasmin that they follow her.

'It wouldn't be the first time I've kissed her,' boasted Jasmin.

He began to tell several ribald tales about her and her friends, so the whole gang, braggarts that we were, followed her down the path, leaving Monsieur Seurel to proceed alone down the road in the donkey cart. But as we came closer to our prey, the group began to fall back, one by one. Even Delouche seemed reluctant to accost the girl in front of all of us. He never got closer to her than fifty metres. So after a few wolf-whistles and some crowing and clucking, we backed off and retraced our steps, feeling uncomfortable. We had to run along the road to catch up with Monsieur Seurel, and we weren't singing any more.

We changed into our swimming costumes under the dry willows on the banks of the Cher. The trees hid us from onlookers, but not from the sun. Hot and sweaty, with our feet on sand or on the dried mud of the river bank, we thought longingly about the widow Delouche's bottle of lemonade, cooling in the spring at Grand'Fons, a spring that bubbled into a pool beside the Cher. At the bottom of the spring, we could see blue-green weeds and two or three creatures resembling woodlice. The water was so pure, so transparent, that fishermen never hesitated to kneel down, with a hand on either side, to drink from it.

Unfortunately, this day went the same way as all the others . . .

When we had changed, we sat down in a circle, cross-legged, to share the cold lemonade from two large glasses, offering Monsieur Seurel the first drink. It didn't occur to us that this little sip would merely prickle our throats and aggravate our thirst. So, one by one we went back to the spring which we had been suspicious of at first, and slowly brought our faces to the surface of the water. But not all of us were used to the ways of country people. Many, including me, could not quench their thirst – some because they did not consider water to be a proper beverage; others because their throats closed up in fear of swallowing a woodlouse; others, deceived by the utmost transparency of the still water, and not knowing how to judge the distance from the surface, submerged their entire faces and inhaled water through their noses, water so cold that seemed to burn; and others for all these reasons at once. No matter. It seemed to us on those dry banks of the Cher that all the coolness of the earth was to be found in this little pool. Even now, at the mere mention of the word 'spring', it is always that pool I remember.

We made our return at dusk, carefree again. The Grand'Fons

path, which climbed up to the road, was a stream in winter, an impassable ravine in summer, full of holes and huge roots, which crawled around in the shadows between rows of trees. Some of the swimmers went up the ravine for a lark. But the rest of us, including Monsieur Seurel and Jasmin, followed the easy, sandy path which ran parallel to it. We could hear the others chatting and laughing near us, below us, invisible in the ravine, while Jasmin continued to boast about his conquests.

From the tops of trees that created what looked like an enormous hedge, we could hear the whir of evening insects and could even pick them out against the sky as they flew above the lacy foliage. Occasionally one would drop from the sky and surprise us with a sudden buzz.

Oh, what a calm and beautiful summer evening it was as we returned, carefree, from the simple pleasures of the countryside. But Jasmin, once again, without meaning to, disturbed our tranquillity.

When we arrived at the crest, at a spot with two huge, old stones (they could have been the vestiges of an ancient castle), he was talking about estates he had visited, especially a half-abandoned one near Vieux-Nançay, called Les Sablonnières. Using the affected accent of the Allier region, which elongates certain words while chopping others short, he recounted having seen, a couple of years previously, a tombstone in the ruined chapel of this property, on which were carved these words:

Here lies the knight of Galois
Faithful to his God, his King, and his Lady

'Hmm. Yes. Well . . .' said Monsieur Seurel, shrugging his shoulders slightly with irritation at the turn the conversation was taking, even though he wanted us to go on conversing like grown men. So Jasmin continued to describe the castle just as if he had lived there all his life.

Several times, coming back from Vieux-Nançay, his uncle

Dumas and he had been intrigued by the old grey turret they could see above the pine trees. They traced it to a maze of derelict buildings in the middle of the woods, which one could explore in the owners' absence. One day, they offered the gamekeeper a lift in their cart, and in return, he gave them a tour of the strange estate. Since then, just about everything had been torn down; all that remained was the farmhouse and a little holiday cottage. The original occupants were still there: a wreck of an old man, who was a retired officer, and his daughter.

Jasmin blathered on and on. I listened attentively, unconsciously aware that what he said concerned something I knew well. Suddenly, simply, in the way of extraordinary revelations, Jasmin was struck by an idea he had never had before.

'Whoa!' he cried, grabbing my arm. 'Isn't that the place where Meaulnes – you know, our very own magnificent Meaulnes – must have gone?'

'Yes,' he continued, because I did not respond. 'I remember the gamekeeper talking about the son of the household, an eccentric who had some weird ideas.'

I didn't listen any more as I was already convinced that he had guessed correctly. Directly in front of me, but far from Meaulnes and all his hopes, lay the route to the lost domain, as straighforward as a familiar path.

CHAPTER II

AT UNCLE FLORENTIN'S

EVEN though I had been a miserable, dreamy, buttoned-up child, I became resolute and decisive once I realised that the outcome of this entire adventure rested on my shoulders.

I believe that my knee ceased hurting from that evening on.

My father's entire family came from Vieux-Nançay, the community attached to the Les Sablonnières estate. We often spent the end of September there with my uncle, Florentin, a merchant; liberated from exams, I couldn't wait to go immediately to my uncle's. But I decided not to let Meaulnes know I would be there until I was certain of giving him happy news. What good would it do to snatch him from sorrow only to plunge him into despair?

I loved Vieux-Nançay better than any place in the world, but our visits were infrequent – just the end of summer holidays and those rare occasions when we could get hold of a carriage to take us there. At one time, a quarrel broke out with a branch of the family living in Vieux-Nançay. This is undoubtedly why each time we had to beg Millie so hard to join us in the carriage. But I couldn't have cared less about these disputes! No sooner had I arrived than I would lose myself in the midst of all the uncles and cousins, totally occupied by the fun to be had and the sheer pleasure of being there.

We would descend on Uncle Florentin and Aunt Julie, who had a son of my age, Firmin, and eight daughters. The eldest two girls, Marie-Louise and Charlotte, must have been seventeen and fifteen years old at the time. The family's large general store was located across from the church, at one of the entrances to this town in the

Sologne, and it supplied all the manor houses and hunting lodges scattered across the sparsely populated landscape, all at least thirty kilometres from any train station.

This shop, with its grocery counter and haberdashery, overlooked the road through numerous windows and the town square through a glass door. Strangely, although it was quite normal in this poor region, the floor consisted of nothing but packed earth.

In the rear were six rooms, each filled with a different kind of merchandise: a hat room; a gardening room; a lamp room, and so on. When I was a child and wandered around in this maze of a bazaar, it seemed I could never exhaust the sight of all those wonders. And even as a young man, I still felt that my only true holidays were spent in this place.

The family practically lived in the big kitchen whose door opened into the shop, a kitchen where flames blazed brightly in the hearth at the end of September, where hunters and poachers, who sold their game to Florentin, came early in the morning for a drink, while the little girls, already up, ran around yelling and dousing their silky hair with eau-de-cologne. On the walls, yellowing photographs showed my father – it took me a while to recognise him in his uniform – in the midst of his comrades at university.

While we were there, we spent our mornings in the kitchen and in the courtyard where Florentin grew dahlias and raised guinea fowl. We roasted coffee, seated on soap boxes, and unpacked cases of all kinds of carefully wrapped, precious objects for which we often had no name.

All day long the shop was overrun with peasants and coachmen from the manor houses. Carriages from the depths of the country would appear out of the September mist, and empty out in front of the glass door. From the kitchen we could hear the peasant women talking, and we eavesdropped eagerly.

But come eight o'clock in the evening, after we had carried hay by lanternlight to the steaming horses in the stables, the whole shop belonged to us!

While Marie-Louise, the eldest of my cousins but one of the smallest, folded and sorted piles of linens, she encouraged us to come and entertain her. Then Firmin and I and all the girls would burst into the large shop, and by the light of the inn's lamps, begin grinding the coffee mills, performing acrobatics on the counter, and sometimes – because the beaten earth was an invitation to dance – Firmin fetched an old trombone covered in verdigris, from the attic, so that he could accompany us.

I still blush at the thought that in previous years, Mademoiselle de Galais could have arrived at this hour on any day and surprised us at our childish games . . . But it wasn't until one evening that particular August, a little before nightfall, while I was chatting with Marie-Louise and Firmin, that I saw her for the first time.

From the evening I arrived at Vieux-Nançay, I had asked Uncle Florentin about Les Sablonnières.

'It's no longer a large estate,' he said. 'It has been sold and the buyers, huntsmen, have torn down the old buildings so as to enlarge their hunting territory. The main courtyard is nothing but a wasteland of heather and gorse. The old owners retained nothing but a little cottage and the farm. You may well have a chance to see Mademoiselle de Galais; she often does the shopping herself – sometimes she comes on horseback, sometimes in a carriage, but always with the same old horse, Bélisaire. They make a comical pair!'

I was so troubled that I had to struggle to ask the next question.

'They were rich, weren't they?'

'Yes. Monsieur de Galais used to give huge parties to entertain his son, a strange boy with some very peculiar ideas. To distract him, the father thought up whatever he could. He even imported playmates for him from Paris and elsewhere . . .

'All of Les Sablonnières lay in ruins, and Madame de Galais was near death, but still they sought to realise their son's fantasies. Last winter, no, the winter before, they gave their biggest costume ball ever. Half the guests came from Paris, half were locals. They bought or hired quantities of marvellous costumes, games, horses, boats, always trying to amuse Frantz de Galais. A rumour went around that he was going to be married and they were celebrating his engagement. But he was too young. Everything fell apart, and he ran away and has never been seen since. The lady of the manor died, and suddenly Mademoiselle de Galais was left alone with her father, the old sea captain.'

'Didn't she marry?' I asked at last.

'No,' he said. 'Not so far as I've heard. Perhaps you'd like to be a suitor!'

Totally disconcerted, I confessed to him, as discreetly as possible, that my best friend, Augustin Meaulnes, might be interested in her.

'Well!' said Florentin, smiling. 'If he's not looking for a wife with money, it could be a good match. Should I talk to Monsieur de Galais about it? He still comes here from time to time to buy buckshot. I always give him a taste of my special brandy.'

I begged him not to do anything just yet. All these happy coincidences worried me, and anxiety held me back from telling Meaulnes anything until I had at least set eyes on the girl.

I didn't have long to wait. The next evening, a little before dinnertime, as night began to fall, a cool mist descended, making it feel more like September than August. Hoping to find the shop empty of customers, Firmin and I were on our way to chat with Marie-Louise and Charlotte. I had told them the secret that had brought me to Vieux-Nançay at this unusually early date. With our elbows on the counter, or seated on it with both hands flat on the polished wood, we were adding up everything we knew about the mysterious young woman – which boiled down to very little – when the sound of wheels made us turn our heads.

'Here she is!' they whispered.

A few seconds later, a strange vehicle drew up in front of the glass doors: an old farm waggon with rounded side panels and moulded roof racks – something we had never seen before in this part of the world – and an ancient white horse who lowered his head to nibble every blade of grass he saw. In the driver's seat, and I say this simply but truthfully, was the most beautiful young woman in the world.

Never had I seen such grace combined with such seriousness. Her outfit exaggerated how slender she was, making her appear fragile. As she entered, she threw off her heavy brown cloak. Her long, blonde hair framed her forehead and delicately modelled face. Her complexion was immaculate, except for a mere two freckles, a gift of the summer sun. I could only find one fault in so much beauty – in moments of sadness, of discouragement, or merely of profound relection, this pure face became lightly mottled with red, as sometimes happens with certain people suffering from a grave but undiagnosed illness. My admiration for her was accompanied by pity, all the more heartrending because it was so surprising.

I took this all in while she was slowly descending from the waggon. At last Marie-Louise introduced us in her easy-going manner, and encouraged me to talk to her.

Someone pulled up a polished chair, and she sat with her back to the counter while the rest of us stood around. She seemed to be quite at home in the shop and to like it. Aunt Julie, alerted to her arrival, bustled in and joined the conversation, her hands crossed over her stomach, nodding her country-shopkeeper's head in its white bonnet, and delaying the moment when the conversation would inevitably turn to me.

I need not have worried because Mademoiselle de Galais spoke to me first.

'So,' she said, 'you will soon become a teacher.'

My aunt lit the porcelain lamp over our heads, giving the shop a feeble light. Admiring the young woman's sweet, childlike face, her blue eyes and open expression, I was surprised by the clarity and gravity of her voice. When she finished speaking, she gazed into the distance, not moving while she waited for a reply, except for biting her lip a little.

'I would teach too, if my father let me. I would like to teach little boys, like your mother does,' she added with a smile as she revealed that my cousins had already talked to her about me.

'The villagers have always been sweet, polite, and helpful, and I love them very much. But their attitude towards a teacher is often quite antagonistic. They quibble and grasp, moaning endlessly about lost pencases and the price of exercise books, and that their children aren't learning anything. Nevertheless, I feel I could win them over. But perhaps this might be more difficult than I imagine.'

Without smiling, but looking thoughtful and childlike, she resumed her steady blue-eyed gaze. We were all a bit embarrassed by the frankness with which she spoke of delicate matters and subtle relationships only mentioned in books, but after a brief silence, we began conversing again.

With a certain animosity towards some mystery in her life, the young woman continued, 'And I would teach the village boys such wisdom as I have learned, but I would not urge them to travel the world, as you will undoubtedly do, young Monsieur Seurel, when you become assistant headmaster. Instead, I would help them find what they cannot perceive at first: happiness close at hand.'

Marie-Louise and Firmin were just as dumbfounded as I was. We remained speechless. Recognising our discomfort, she stopped, bit her lip, lowered her head, and then smiled in a teasing way.

'So,' she said, 'perhaps there is a certain tall, crazy, young man who is looking for me at the ends of the world while I sit right here in Madame Florentin's shop, under this light, with my old horse waiting outside the door. If the young man saw me here, he wouldn't believe his eyes.'

Her smile emboldened me to laugh and say, 'And what if I know this crazy young man?'

She eyed me sharply.

At this moment, the doorbell rang, and two women entered, carrying baskets.

'Come into the dining room, where you won't be disturbed,' said my aunt to Mademoiselle de Galais, pushing open the kitchen door. But she refused and insisted on leaving right away, so my aunt added as an inducement, 'Your father is here, chatting with Florentin in front of the fire.'

Even in the month of August, a pine log burned and crackled in the kitchen hearth, and the porcelain lamp was lit too. Seated beside Florentin was an old man with a kindly face, clean-shaven and hollow-cheeked, and almost entirely silent, as though weighed down by age and memories. In front of them stood two glasses of *marc*.

'François!' my uncle shouted at me as if a river or several acres of land separated us, 'I have just organised an afternoon of pleasure on the banks of the Cher next Thursday. Some of us will hunt, others will fish, some will dance, and others will swim. Mademoiselle, you will come on horseback. Monsieur de Galais has agreed. I've arranged everything. And François,' he added, as if he had only just thought of it, 'you can bring your friend Meaulnes. That's his name, isn't it?'

Mademoiselle de Galais stood up, suddenly very pale. At that very moment, I remembered that Meaulnes told her his name when they were talking near the pond in the lost domain.

She held out her hand to me in parting, and I took it, our touch expressing more clearly than if we had spoken a secret understanding that only death would destroy, and a friendship more moving than a grand passion.

At four o'clock the following morning, Firmin knocked on the door of the little room in the courtyard that I shared with his guinea fowl. It was still night and a challenge to find my things on the table, encumbered as it was with objects such as brass chandeliers and statuettes of saints, which Aunt Julie had brought out from the shop on the eve of my arrival to decorate the room for me. In the courtyard, I could hear my uncle inflating my bicycle tyres, and my aunt blowing on the fire in the kitchen. The sun was just rising as I left. The day would be long; I planned to go first to Sainte-Agathe to explain my prolonged absence before continuing on to La Ferté-d'Angillon. I would arrive before evening at the home of my friend, Augustin Meaulnes.

CHAPTER III

AN APPARITION

FOR a long time, in secret, and in spite of my bad knee, Jasmin had been teaching me how to ride a bicycle, but this was the first time I had made a long journey. If a bicycle is an exciting vehicle for an ordinary young man, how much more so it seems for a poor boy like me who, a short time before, had dragged his leg and became soaked with sweat after a short walk. To swoop into the depths of the countryside from high crests; to discover, as if with the flap of a wing, distant roads opening up and coming into focus at my approach; to cross a village in the blink of an eye, but taking it all in. Only in dreams did I have such delightful experiences. Even cycling uphill did not daunt me. I felt almost drunk with pleasure that day in late August as I pedalled along the road leading to Meaulnes's part of the country.

'A little before entering town,' Meaulnes had said when he described the route to me, 'you will see a large wheel with blades to catch the wind.' He did not know the purpose of this wheel, or perhaps he pretended not to know in order to sharpen my curiosity.

Early that evening at the end of August, I came upon an immense meadow, and caught sight of the huge wheel turning in the wind, lifting up water for a neighbouring farm. Behind the poplars at the end of the meadow, I could see a few houses on the outskirts of town. As I followed a long detour that skirted the river, the vista opened up, and when I arrived at the bridge, I found myself on the main street of the village.

I could hear cowbells jangling as the animals grazed, hidden by meadow reeds. I dismounted and, with both hands on the handle-bars, surveyed the scene where I was about to deliver such important news. The houses were lined up along the edge of a ditch, each linked to the road by a wooden bridge. They looked like barges, their sails folded, moored in the calm of the evening, at the time of day when a fire was lit in each kitchen.

But fear and an unwillingness to disturb so much peace began to eat away at my courage. Just then, to aggravate my sudden hesitation, I remembered that an aunt on the Moinel side of my family also lived in La Ferté-d'Angillon, in one of its little squares.

She was actually a great-aunt. All her children were dead, but I had known Ernest, the youngest, very well. He was a big fellow with plans to be a teacher. My great-uncle Moinel, the old clerk of the court, swiftly followed him to the grave, leaving my aunt alone in her strange little house, where the carpets were made of scraps sewn together, where the tables were covered in paper cutouts of roosters, hens, and cats, where the walls were plastered with old diplomas, portraits of the deceased, and lockets made from the curls of the dear departed.

Even in these sad surroundings, she personified eccentricity and good humour. When I found her house in the square, I called to her loudly from the open front door, and heard her give a sharp cry from three rooms back:

'Good God!'

She tipped her coffee into the fire – what on earth was she doing with coffee at that hour? – and appeared in front of me, her shoulders thrown back. On her head, she wore a sort of hooded cap over her wide, protuberant forehead, giving her the look of a Mongolian, or perhaps even a Hottentot. She cackled with laughter, revealing what remained of her pointed teeth.

While I was embracing her, she awkwardly grabbed hold of the hand behind my back. With unneccessary stealth, since we were completely alone, she slipped me a coin which I dared not look at but guessed was a franc . . . Then, seeing I wanted to express my thanks, she gave me a quick shove and cried:

'Go on, then! I know what it's like to be poor.'

She had always been poor, forever borrowing, forever spending. 'I've always been stupid and always unfortunate,' she would squeak without bitterness.

Believing that I was just as preoccupied with money as she was, the good lady did not wait for me to draw a breath before hiding in my hand the slim savings of her day. From then on, that was how she always greeted me.

Dinner was just as peculiar as the greeting, sad and bizarre at the same time. She kept a candle at hand, but sometimes wandered away with it, leaving me in the dark, and other times she placed it on a side table which was covered with chipped and cracked dishes and vases.

'The Prussians broke the handles of this one back in sixty-six. It was too big for them to carry off.'

Only then, when I looked at the huge vase with its tragic history, did I remember that my father and I had dined and slept at her house long ago. He was taking me to a knee specialist in Yonne, and we had to catch an express train which came through La Ferté before daybreak. I recalled that dreary dinner and the long stories the old clerk told, sitting in front of a glass of rosé with his elbows on the table.

And I also remembered my terrors. After dinner, seated in front of the fire, my great-aunt took my father aside to tell him a ghost story: 'I turn around . . . Ah! my poor Louis, what do I see, a little grey woman . . .' It was well known that my aunt had a head full of terrifying twaddle.

So there I was, after dinner that evening, tired out from my bicycle ride, wearing one of my Uncle Moinel's checked nightshirts, settled in bed in the large bedroom, when my aunt came and sat beside me and began to talk in her most mysterious and shrill voice.

'My dear François, I must tell you something I have never told anyone.'

'I've had it,' I thought. 'She's going to terrify me out of my wits again and I won't be able to sleep a wink, just like the last time, ten years ago.'

But I had to listen. She nodded her head, and looked straight ahead as if she was recounting the story to herself.

'I was coming back from a party with Moinel. It was the first wedding we had gone to together since the death of our poor Ernest, and I ran across my sister Adèle there, whom I hadn't seen for four years. One of Moinel's old friends had invited us to the wedding of his son at Les Sablonnières. We had hired a coach, which cost a lot of money. We came home along the road at about seven o'clock in the morning. It was midwinter, and the sun was just rising – absolutely no one around. Suddenly, what do I see in front of us on the road? A short young man as beautiful as day, stock-still, watching us come towards him. As we approached, we could make out his pretty face, so white and so pretty that it frightened us.

'I took Moinel's arm. I was trembling like a leaf because I thought it was the good Lord. I said to Moinel: "Look! It's a ghost!" And he replied in a low voice, furiously, "Be quiet, you old chatterbox! I've seen it too!"

'He didn't know what to do. The horse stopped. Up close, we could see how pale the young man's face was, his sweating forehead, dirty beret, and long trousers. Then we heard a sweet voice saying:

'"I am not a man. I am a young girl. I ran away, but I can go no further. Please, I beg you, give me a lift in your carriage, kind sir."

'We immediately invited her on board. Right after she sat down, she lost consciousness. Can you guess who it was? It was the fiancée of Frantz de Galais, the young man from Les Sablonnières to whose wedding we had been invited.'

'But there can't have been a wedding,' I said, 'since the fiancée had run away.'

'Well, no,' she agreed. 'There was no wedding. This unfortunate girl, Valentine, the daughter of a poor weaver, was full of crazy ideas, and she poured out everything. She had become convinced that such a wealth of happiness was not possible in life; that the young man was just that, too young for her; that all the marvels he had described were imaginary. When at last Frantz arrived to claim her, he took her and her older sister for a walk in the Archbishop's garden in Bourges, even though it was cold and windy. The young man, out of politeness, paid a good deal of attention to the sister, even though it was Valentine he loved. Her imagination went wild, and she took fright. She announced that she was going to fetch a scarf from the house. There, she changed into men's clothes so as not to be recognised, and left on foot on the road to Paris.

'Her fiancé received a letter from her in which she declared that she was going to join another young man whom she loved. It wasn't true.

'"I am more happy about my sacrifice," she told me, "than if I was his wife." Poor fool. He certainly had no intention of marrying her sister. He was so distressed that he pulled a pistol on himself – they found his blood in the woods, but have never recovered his body.'

'What did you do with this unfortunate girl?'

'When we reached home, we gave her something to drink. Then we gave her something to eat, and then she slept in front of the fire. She stayed with us for a good part of the winter. From dawn to dusk, she cut out and sewed dresses, fixed hats, and cleaned the house furiously. It was she who repaired all the upholstery you see over there. And since her stay here, the swallows have nested outdoors. But in the evening, at nightfall, with her work finished, she always found a pretext to go out into the courtyard, into the garden, or on to the doorstep, even if it was cold enough to crack stone. And we would find her standing there, crying with all her heart.

'"Well, what's the matter? Tell me," I would beg her.

'"Nothing, Madame Moinel!" And she would come back inside.

'The neighbours started talking: "You have found a pretty little maid, Madame Moinel."

'In spite of our supplications to stay, she resumed her journey to Paris in the month of March. I gave her some dresses which she had

mended. Moinel bought her ticket at the station and gave her a little
money.

'She did not forget us. She is a dressmaker in Paris now, near
Notre-Dame. She often wrote to us asking if we knew what was
going on at Les Sablonnières. Finally, to free her from this obsession,
I replied that the estate had been sold, torn down, that the young
man had disappeared for good, and that the young girl had married.
All that must be true, I think. Since that time, my Valentine has
written far less frequently.'

Even though Aunt Moinel was not recounting a ghost story in her
strident little voice, so well suited to such stories, I was filled with
apprehension. Had we not sworn that we would serve Frantz, our
gypsy, like brothers? Was this not the perfect opportunity to do
just that?

On the other hand, telling Frantz what I had just learned would
kill the joy I intended to bring to Meaulnes the following morning.
What good would it do to launch him into a perfectly impossible
enterprise? Yes, we had the young girl's address, but how could we
find the gypsy who was running all over the world? Let fools be
fools, I thought. Delouche and Boujardon were right. This wildly
romantic Frantz had brought us nothing but misfortune. I resolved
to keep quiet until I had done everything in my power to ensure
that Augustin Meaulnes and Mademoiselle de Galais were safely
married.

Having taken this decision, I still suffered a feeling of foreboding
– a feeling I quickly tried to banish as ridiculous.

The candle had almost burned down. A mosquito droned. But
Aunt Moinel, elbows on her knees, head resting on the velvet cape
that she only took off when she went to bed, resumed her story.
Occasionally, she lifted her head sharply and looked at me to gauge
my impressions, or to make sure that I had not gone to sleep. Finally,
with my head on the pillow, I deceitfully closed my eyes and
pretended to doze off.

'Look at this! You're sleeping,' she said in a less shrill but somewhat disappointed voice.

I felt sorry for her, and protested, 'No, dear aunt, I assure you . . .'

'But, yes!' she said. 'I knew all along that all this could hardly interest you. After all, I have been speaking about people you never knew.'

This time, coward that I was, I did not reply.

CHAPTER IV

EXCITING NEWS

WHEN I arrived on the main street the next morning, it was such a beautiful, calm summer's day and the whole town was so full of peaceful, early-morning sounds, that I regained the joyous confidence of a bearer of good tidings.

Augustin and his mother lived in an old schoolhouse. On the death of his father, who had been retired for a long time, Meaulnes, wealthy because of an inheritance, decided to buy the school where the old instructor had taught for twenty years, and where he himself had learned to read. He did not buy it because it was a handsome house; it was a huge, square building that looked like a town hall, and had, in fact, been just that. The ground floor windows were placed so high that no one could peer in them from the street, and the empty courtyard in the rear – the barest, most desolate schoolyard that I had ever seen – sported an awning that blocked out the view of the countryside.

I found Augustin's mother in the tortuous four-doored corridor, bringing in a huge load of laundry which she must have hung out to dry in the early hours of this long holiday morning. Her grey hair was dishevelled, and wisps of it floated around her head. Her face looked puffy and tired, as though she had been awake all night, and she wore a sad and pensive air.

Glancing up suddenly, she recognised me, and smiled.

'You're just in time,' she said. 'I'm bringing in the last laundry before Augustin's departure. I spent the night settling his accounts and organising his business affairs. The train leaves at five o'clock, but everything should be ready by then.'

Because she was so explicit, I began to feel that she herself had made Augustin's decision to leave, even though she seemed to have no idea where he was actually going.

'Go upstairs,' she said, 'you will find him in the mayor's office, writing something.

I hurriedly climbed the stairs, opened the door on the right which still proclaimed it was the mayor's office, and found myself in a large room, its walls decorated with yellowing portraits of presidents Grévy and Carnot. Of its four windows, two faced the town and two faced the countryside. On a long dais which took up the far end of the room, the municipal councillors' chairs still stood in front of a table with a green cloth. Meaulnes sat in the mayor's armchair, writing at the table, dipping his pen now and then into the bottom of an old-fashioned faience inkwell shaped like a heart. During the long vacation, Meaulnes often retreated to this place – perfect for someone leading a life of leisure – when he was not out roaming the countryside.

He rose when he heard me come in, but not as eagerly as I had hoped, saying only 'Seurel!' with an air of profound astonishment.

He was still the same big fellow – the same bony face, the same shaved head, the same direct gaze. But now an unkempt moustache sprouted above his lip, and a mist-like veil over his eyes dimmed the passionate ardour of past years.

He seemed bewildered by my presence. In one bound, I leaped on to the dais, but strange to say, he didn't even hold out his hand. Instead, he turned towards me, his hands behind his back, and propped himself against the table, extremely ill at ease. He gazed into the middle distance, preparing what to say. He was always slow to start conversations – like hunters and adventurers and most people who live alone – and he would make a decision without worrying about how he would express it. Now that I was in front of him, he began to search for the necessary words of explanation.

In the meantime, I cheerfully told him about my journey, where I had spent the night, and how surprised I was to find Madame Meaulnes preparing for his departure.

'She told you about it?' he asked.

'Yes. I don't imagine you are going away for long?'

'Yes, I am. It's a very long trip.'

Disconcerted, feeling that one word from me could nullify a decision I did not understand, I could no longer hold back my news, even though I did not know how to begin.

He beat me to it, speaking this time like someone who wanted to justify himself.

'Seurel,' he said, 'the strange adventure while I was at Sainte-Agathe became my reason for living and for hope. When I lost that hope, what could I do? How could I go on living like everyone else?

'I realised that everything was finished and there was no more point in looking for the lost estate, so I tried to live in Paris. But once a man has visited paradise, how can he readjust to the world? Other people's happiness seemed ridiculous. And when one day I decided sincerely, deliberately to behave like everyone else, I accumulated a lifetime of remorse.'

Seated on a chair on the dais with my head lowered, I listened without looking at him, with no idea where his incomprehensible explanation was going.

'Come on, Meaulnes,' I said, 'explain yourself more clearly! Why the long journey? Do you have some wrong to right? A promise to keep?'

'Well, yes,' he replied. 'You remember the promise I made to Frantz?'

'Aah!' I sighed with relief. 'Is that all it is?'

'That's it, and a wrong to right too. Both at the same time.'

I decided it was my turn to speak, and began to prepare my words. But he started up again

'There is only one real explanation. Certainly, I would have liked to see Mademoiselle de Galais once more, just to lay eyes on her. But I am persuaded now that when I entered that nameless domain, I was at a height of perfection and purity that I will never attain again. As I once wrote to you, only in death will I regain the beauty of that moment.'

He drew close, and his voice changed as he started up again with burning intensity.

'Listen, Seurel! This new scheme of mine, this long journey, and my need to right the wrong I did, are in a sense the continuation of my old adventure.'

He paused, painfully trying to recapture his memories. Having missed the previous opportunity to speak, I could not let this one escape. At last, I spoke up – too quickly, because I later bitterly regretted not having given him enough time to make his full confession.

I pronounced the words I had prepared, but they were no longer valid. Without gesturing, and barely lifting my head, I said:

'What if I were to tell you that all hope was not lost?'

He looked at me, then turning his eyes quickly away, blushed redder than I have ever seen anyone blush, a huge rush of blood to his temples.

'What are you saying?' he asked in a small voice.

Then, in one huge breath, I told him what I knew, what I had done, and how, with everything changed, it felt as though Yvonne de Galais herself had sent me to him.

He was now frighteningly pale.

He listened to my entire story in silence, his head turned back towards me, in the attitude of someone who has been surprised and does not know how to defend himself, whether to hide or to flee. He interrupted me only once, when I added that Les Sablonnières had been demolished and the estate he remembered no longer existed as such.

'Ah, you see . . .' he said, as if he had been on the lookout for an opening to justify his behaviour and mitigate the despair into which he had sunk. 'You see, there's nothing left . . .'

Convinced that the great opportunity we were offering him would make him feel better, I finished by telling him that my uncle Florentin had organised a picnic in the country to which Mademoiselle de Galais was going on her horse, and that he himself had been invited. But he appeared to be completely bewildered and made no reply.

'You must cancel your trip immediately,' I said impatiently. 'Let's go and tell your mother.'

While we were going downstairs together, he said hesitantly:

'This picnic in the country . . . Do I really have to go?'

'What a stupid question!'

He looked like someone being shoved along by the shoulders.

Downstairs, Augustin alerted Madame Meaulnes that I would be lunching with them, dining with them, and spending the night. The following morning he would borrow a bicycle and follow me to Vieux-Nançay.

'Very well,' she said, nodding her head, as if this news had confirmed her expectations.

I sat down in the little dining room, under the illustrated calendars, the ornamental daggers, and the Sudanese wineskins that Monsieur Meaulnes's brother, previously a soldier in the marine infantry, had brought back from his distant travels.

Augustin left me in the dining room for a moment before we ate lunch. In the adjoining room, where his mother had packed his luggage, I heard him tell her softly not to unpack his trunk because it was possible that his journey was merely postponed.

CHAPTER V

A PLEASURE TRIP

IT was impossible to keep up with Augustin on the road to Vieux-Nançay. He set off like a racing cyclist, and did not dismount even when going uphill. Yesterday's unexpected hesitation was succeeded by nervous excitement and determination to move ahead as quickly as possible, which frightened me somewhat. At my uncle's house, he showed the same impatience; he seemed incapable of concentrating on anything until ten o'clock the following morning when we were all installed in the carriage, ready to leave for the banks of the Cher.

It was the end of August, and summer was waning. Empty husks from yellow chestnut trees already littered the white roads. The journey was short; the farm belonging to the Aubiers was scarcely two kilometres beyond Les Sablonnières, near the point on the Cher where we were to gather. Here and there we ran into other guests in their carriages, and even some young people on horseback whom Florentin had boldly invited in Monsieur de Galais's name. As before, there was a fine mix of people – rich and poor, squire and peasant – and we even saw Jasmin Delouche arriving on his bicycle. Thanks to Baladier, the gamekeeper, he had made my uncle's acquaintance a short while before.

'Here he is, the one who held the key to everything, while we were searching as far as Paris!' growled Meaulnes. 'It's enough to make one weep.'

Each time he looked at Jasmin, his rancour deepened. Delouche, on the other hand, believing that we were in his debt, escorted our carriage as closely as he could. We could see that he had tried, with scant success, to clean himself up, but the threadbare tails of his jacket kept flapping on the mudguard of his bicycle.

In spite of his efforts to be agreeable, his little-old-man's face remained unpleasing. Moreover, he inspired in me a slight feeling of pity. But for whom did I not feel pity during that particular day?

I can never remember that excursion without feelings of regret and suffocation. I had looked forward to the day so much, and everything had been perfectly devised for our happiness, but we were happy for such a short while.

How beautiful the river banks were! We paused on a verge, and the hillside sloped gently down to green meadows and willow groves separated by fences, like so many tiny gardens. On the other side of the river, the banks became grey hills, steep and rocky, and on the furthest hills, we could see romantic castle turrets among the fir trees. From time to time, we heard the hounds of Préveranges castle, baying way off in the distance.

We arrived at the river via a maze of paths, sometimes shingly, sometimes sandy – paths which could suddenly become transformed into streams. As we walked, branches from wild currant bushes snatched at our sleeves. Sometimes we plunged into the cool shade of ravines; other times, when the hedges allowed, we bathed in the bright light of the entire valley. As we approached, we could see a man fishing patiently, crouched on the rocks of the opposite bank. My God, how beautiful it all was!

We installed ourselves on some well-mown grass set back from a stand of birch trees, a place perfectly suited for endless games.

The carriages were unhitched, and the horses led to the Aubiers farm. We started to unpack the provisions and set up folding tables my uncle had brought along.

We needed volunteers to go to the junction to make sure that late arrivals took the right path. I set off. Meaulnes followed me, and we set up our post near the suspension bridge at the crossroads of several paths and the larger road which came from Les Sablonnières.

We waited, walking up and down, speaking of the past, trying as hard as we could to distract ourselves. Another carriage from Vieux-Nançay arrived, bearing several unknown peasants and a tall, beribboned girl. Then nothing, except for three children in a donkey cart, the children of the old gardener at Les Sablonnières.

'I think I recognise them,' said Meaulnes. 'They are the ones who took me by the hand and led me in to dinner on the first night of the celebrations.'

Right then the donkey refused to budge, and the children climbed down from the cart to poke it, pull it, and beat it as hard as they could. Meaulnes, disappointed, claimed he was mistaken.

I asked them if they had encountered Monsieur and Mademoiselle de Galais on the road. One replied that he did not know them. Another said, 'I think we did, sir,' which didn't help much. Eventually they went down towards the lawn, some pulling the donkey by its bridle, others pushing the cart from behind. We remained on watch. Meaulnes gazed at the curve in the road from Les Sablonnières, nervously anticipating the arrival of the young woman he had previously searched for so passionately. A bizarre, almost comical kind of irritation seized him, and he focused this emotion on Jasmin Delouche. We had climbed a small embankment to look as far as possible along the road, and a group of guests was also visible behind us on the grass. Delouche was doing his best to impress them.

'Look at that fool pontificating,' said Meaulnes.

'Leave him alone. He's doing his best, poor boy.'

Augustin did not yield. Then a hare or a squirrel emerged from a thicket, and Jasmin made a show of chasing it.

'Will you look at that! He's running now!' said Meaulnes, as if this were the most arrogant act in the world.

I couldn't help laughing. Meaulnes couldn't either, but only for a moment.

After another fifteen minutes of staring at the road, he said, 'What if she doesn't come?'

'But she promised. Be patient!' I replied.

He continued looking until he couldn't stand the suspense any longer, then said, 'Listen. I'm going to join the others. It's impossible she'll suddenly appear at the end of the road. I know she won't come any time soon if I stay here.'

So he set off towards the lawn, leaving me alone. I walked a few hundred metres along the little road to pass the time. At the first turning, I saw Yvonne de Galais riding sidesaddle on her old white horse. Even he felt frisky this morning, and she was obliged to rein him in to prevent him from trotting. Monsieur de Galais walked at the horse's head in silence, painfully. No doubt they took turns walking and riding.

When the girl saw me alone, she smiled, jumped nimbly to the ground and, handing over the reins to her father, made her way towards me as I was hurrying towards her.

'I'm so happy to find you alone,' she said, 'because I don't want anyone but you to see my old Bélisaire, and I certainly don't want to tether him beside the other horses. He is too old and too ugly, and I'm always afraid he'll get kicked and injured. He's the only horse I dare mount, and when he dies, I won't ride any more.'

Under her charming vivacity, her gracefulness, and apparent peacefulness, I sensed the same impatience and anxiety I felt in Meaulnes. She talked faster than normal and was deathly pale, except for two spots of colour on her cheeks.

We tethered Bélisaire in a little wood beside the road, old Monsieur de Galais silently attaching the beast a bit lower than I thought he should. I promised to order hay, barley, and straw from the farm. Mademoiselle de Galais walked out on to the lawn and then ventured down to the edge of the lake, where Meaulnes caught sight of her for the first time.

Taking her father's arm, spreading out with her left hand a portion of the big, light coat that enveloped her, she moved towards the guests with an expression both serious and childlike. I walked near her. All the guests, who were scattered around playing games, gathered together to greet her, watching her approach in silence.

Meaulnes stood in the middle of a group of young men, with nothing distinguishing him from his companions but his height, although several young fellows were nearly as tall. He did nothing to draw attention to himself, not a gesture, not a step forward. There he stood, dressed in grey, motionless, gawping (like all the others) at the incredibly beautiful young woman who was approaching. Finally, with an unconscious and awkward movement, he placed his hand on his bare head, shaven like a peasant's, as if to conceal himself in the middle of his companions and their well-groomed hair.

The group moved to surround Mademoiselle de Galais, and they introduced her to the young men and women she did not know. Then it was my companion's turn. I was consumed with anxiety, so I decided to make the introduction myself.

But before I could say anything, the young woman advanced towards him with surprising confidence.

'I recognise Augustin Meaulnes,' she said.

And she held out her hand to him.

CHAPTER VI

THE PLEASURE TRIP, PART II

ALMOST immediately, others arrived to greet Yvonne de Galais, so the two young people were separated, and unfortunately they were not seated at the same table for lunch. But Meaulnes seemed to have regained his confidence and courage. I was also separated from him, seated between Delouche and Monsieur de Galais, but several times I caught his eye, and he waved at me across the distance.

Towards the end of the evening, when games, swimming, conversations, and excursions by boat on the neighbouring pond were in full swing, Meaulnes finally found himself in the presence of the young woman. He and I were chatting with Delouche, seated on some garden chairs we had brought along, when Mademoiselle de Galais approached, deliberately leaving a group of young men who seemed to be annoying her. I remember she asked why we were not canoeing on the pond like some of the others.

'We made several rounds this afternoon,' I replied. 'But it was rather monotonous and we quickly tired of it.'

'Well, why don't you go on the river?' she said.

'The current is too strong, and we could be swept away.'

'We need a motorboat or an old-fashioned steamboat,' said Meaulnes.

'We don't have ours any more. We sold it,' she said softly.

An uncomfortable silence followed. Jasmin took advantage of it to announce that he was going in search of Monsieur de Galais.

'I know exactly where to find him,' he said.

What a strange thing! Those two people, such utterly different types, liked each other and had hardly been apart since morning. Monsieur de Galais had even taken me aside at the beginning of the evening to inform me that my friend was full of tact, deference, and other good qualities. Perhaps he had even told Jasmin about Bélisaire and where we had hidden him.

I thought about heading off too, but the two young people seemed so hot and bothered as they faced each other that I decided to stay.

Jasmin's discretion and my caution were of little help, even though they did manage to talk a bit. But invariably, with a stubborness of which he was unaware, Meaulnes kept alluding to the former marvellous times. Each time, Yvonne de Galais painfully reminded him that everything had disappeared: the strange and complex old building, torn down; the big pond, dried up and filled in; and the children in their charming costumes, scattered.

'Ah,' said Meaulnes despairingly, as if each of these disappearances only proved him right.

We were walking side by side. I tried in vain to divert the sadness that had crept over us. With an abrupt question, Meaulnes started up again. He asked about everything he had seen: the little girls, the driver of the old berlin, the racing ponies. 'Have the ponies been sold too? Are there no longer any horses at the estate?'

She replied that there weren't. She didn't mention Bélisaire.

Then he conjured up the objects in his room: the candelabra, the big mirror, the broken lute. He asked about all this with unusual passion, as if he wished to persuade himself that something might have survived from his beautiful adventure, that the young girl might be able to bring him back a piece of flotsam to prove that they had not both been dreaming, the way a diver brings back a pebble and some seaweed from the bottom of the sea.

Mademoiselle de Galais and I could not prevent ourselves from smiling sadly. She decided to elaborate.

'You will never again see the beautiful castle that my father and I fixed up for poor Frantz. We spent our life doing what Frantz demanded. He was such a strange creature, so charming. But everything disappeared on the night of his broken engagement.

'We didn't know it, but my father was already ruined. Frantz had incurred debts, and his old comrades – learning about his disappearance – immediately started making claims on us, which reduced us to poverty. We lost all our friends in a few short days, and then my mother died.

'Oh that Frantz would return, if he is not dead! Oh, that he would regain his friends and his fiancée! That the interrupted wedding would take place, and that everything would be as before! But can the past ever be recaptured?'

'Who knows?' said Meaulnes pensively, and he asked no more questions.

All three of us walked quietly on the short grass, which was already yellowing. The young woman, whom Augustin thought he had lost for ever, walked on his right. When he asked one of his difficult questions, she turned slowly towards him as she responded, with an anxious look on her charming face. Once, while speaking to him, she put her hand gently on his arm, lightly and confidingly. Three years earlier, he would have been driven nearly mad by such good fortune, so why did he behave like a stranger now, like someone who has not found his prize, someone no longer interested in anything? Why this emptiness, this inability to be happy?

We approached the little wood where Monsieur de Galais had tethered Bélisaire that morning. The declining sun lengthened our shadows on the grass. At the other end of the lawn, we heard a happy buzzing sound. It was the voices of young people playing games, muffled by distance. We stayed silent in this lovely calm until we heard someone singing on the other side of the wood, in the direction of Aubiers, the farm at the edge of the water. It was the faraway voice of a young man taking his animals to the drinking trough, singing a dance tune, which he stretched out like a sad ballad:

My shoes are red
Goodbye, my loves
My shoes are red
Goodbye for ever.

Meaulnes raised his head and listened. It was one of the airs that the peasants had sung – those who lingered at the domain after everything had collapsed on the final evening of the celebrations – a paltry jolt to the memory of beautiful days that would never come again.

'Do you hear him?' asked Meaulnes. 'I'm going to see who it is.' Right away he set off into the little wood. Almost immediately the voice was quiet, but one could still hear a second man whistling to his beasts as he drew away. Then nothing.

I looked at the young girl. Thoughtful and overcome, she had her eyes fixed on the copse where Meaulnes had just disappeared. How many times, later on, would she look pensively at the route on which Meaulnes set off for ever!

She turned towards me:

'He is unhappy,' she said sadly, adding, 'Perhaps I can do nothing for him any more.'

I hesitated to reply, believing that Meaulnes, having arrived at the farm in no time, was even now coming back through the wood and might overhear our conversation. But I encouraged her anyway, telling her not to be scared of chivvying him along; that he was dogged by a secret he could never willingly confide to her – or to anyone. Suddenly a cry came from the other side of the wood. Then we heard stamping, like a horse pawing the ground, and voices shouting in dispute. Immediately I realised something had happened to old Bélisaire, and I ran towards the source of the uproar. Mademoiselle de Galais followed at a distance. We must have been seen by people at the end of the lawn because just as I entered the wood, I heard footsteps running in our direction.

Tethered too low, old Bélisaire had one of his front legs tangled in the rope. He had not moved until Monsieur de Galais and Delouche startled him in the course of their walk. Overexcited by the oats he had eaten, he bucked furiously. The two men tried to free him, so clumsily they only snarled him up even more, while narrowly avoiding some dangerous kicks. At that very moment, Meaulnes ran into the group on his way back from Aubiers. Maddened by so much ineptitude, he shoved the two men away so hard they almost rolled into the bushes. In one deft motion, he freed Bélisaire. But it was too late because the harm was already done. The horse must have sprained or broken something; he trembled violently, his head hung low, his saddle was loose on his back, and he pulled one leg up against his belly in a pitiful manner. Meaulnes crouched down and examined him without a word.

When he looked up, he saw no one, even though we were all gathered round him. He was red-faced with anger.

'Who on earth tethered him like this? And left his saddle on his back all day long? And who dared to ride this old horse, good at most for dragging a cart?'

Delouche started to speak – he wanted to take it on himself.

'Shut up!' said Meaulnes. 'It's your fault. I saw you stupidly yanking on his tether to untie him.'

Looking down again, he began to rub the horse's hock with the flat of his hand.

Monsieur de Galais, who hadn't spoken until then, made the mistake of breaking the silence.

'Naval officers usually . . . My horse . . . ' he stammered.

'Ah! So it's your horse?' said Meaulnes, a little more calmly but still red with anger as he turned towards the old man.

I thought he would change his tone and make an apology. He hesitated for a moment, but then I saw him take bitter pleasure in making a bad situation worse, smashing and damaging it for ever.

'I cannot offer you my compliments,' he sneered.

'Perhaps some cool water,' someone suggested. 'Take him down to the ford.'

Without acknowledging the suggestion, Meaulnes announced, 'This old horse must be taken away immediately, while he can still walk. There is no time to lose. He must be confined to his stable.'

Several young men offered to help. Mademoiselle de Galais thanked them hurriedly, and then, her face on fire, ready to burst into tears, she said goodbye to everyone, even Meaulnes who was so disconcerted that he did not dare look at her. She took Bélisaire by the reins, as if she were giving him her hand, more to bring him close to her than to lead him. The end-of-summer wind was so mild on the path to Les Sablonnières that it could have been May, with the leaves trembling in the breeze from the south. We saw her go, one arm half out of her coat, holding the heavy leather rein in her tiny hand. Her father walked painfully beside her.

What a sad end to the evening! Little by little, people picked up their bundles and utensils. They folded the chairs and took down the tables. One by one, the coaches left, filled with baggage and people raising their hats and waving their handkerchiefs. A few stayed behind with my uncle Florentin, who, like the rest of us did not speak, but reflected on his regrets and huge disappointment.

Then we left, swiftly carried away in his carriage with its good suspension, drawn by the beautiful chestnut horse. The wheels squeaked as we turned in the sand, and soon Meaulnes and I, looking back at the crossroads from the rear seat, watched as the entrance to the path old Bélisaire and his owners had taken disappeared.

Then my companion – the person most unlikely to cry in the world – turned suddenly towards me, his eyes welling with tears. Then he placed his hand on Florentin's shoulder and said:

'Please stop. Don't worry about me. I would like to go home alone, on foot.'

He put his hand on the mudguard of the carriage, and with one bound jumped to the ground. To our amazement, he began to retrace his steps, running as far as the path we had just passed, the path to Les Sablonnières. It would take him to the domain by the same avenue of pine trees where he, a vagabond hidden among the low-hanging branches, had overheard the mysterious conversation among beautiful, unknown children.

That evening, sobbing his heart out, he asked Mademoiselle de Galais to marry him.

CHAPTER VII

THE WEDDING DAY

IT is a Thursday at the beginning of February, a beautiful, icy afternoon, with a strong wind blowing. Half past three . . . four o'clock. Since noon, laundry draped on hedges all over town has been drying in the gusts. In each house, the fire in the dining room illuminates a whole array of toys. Tired of playing with them, the child sits down next to his mother and makes her tell him about her wedding day.

For someone who does not wish to feel so settled, there are alternatives. He can climb into the attic and stay there until nightfall listening to the wind whistling and groaning, imagining shipwrecks; or he can go outside on to the road, and the wind will blow his scarf into his open mouth, like a sudden warm kiss. But should he wish to witness the happiness of others, he can find it in the house at Les Sablonnières, on the edge of a muddy track, the house my friend Meaulnes returned to with Yvonne de Galais. She has been his wife since noon.

The engagement lasted five months. It was as peaceful as their first encounter had been turbulent. Meaulnes went often to Les Sablonnières, on his bicycle or by coach. Two or three times a week, as Mademoiselle de Galais sat sewing or reading near the big window overlooking the moorland and the pine forest, she would suddenly see his tall silhouette pass rapidly in front of the curtain. He always came by the roundabout way he took the first time. But this was the only allusion – silent – that he made to the past. His happiness seemed to have put his torment to rest.

Some little events stand out from those five months. I became the teacher in the hamlet of Saint-Benoist-des-Champs. Saint-Benoist isn't even a village. It is a collection of farms scattered across the countryside, and the school house is completely isolated on a hillside although it is near the road. I lead a very solitary life, but if I take a shortcut through the fields, it is only a forty-five-minute walk to Les Sablonnières.

Delouche is living with his uncle, a building contractor at Vieux-Nançay. He will soon be the boss. He comes to see me frequently. Thanks to Mademoiselle de Galais's entreaties, Meaulnes has become very friendly with him.

This explains how we are both there, wandering about towards four o'clock in the afternoon, even though the rest of the wedding party has all left.

The marriage took place as quietly as possible, in the ancient chapel at Les Sablonnières, which still stands, half-hidden by the pine trees on nearby slopes. After a quick lunch, Augustin's mother, Monsieur Seurel and Millie, Florentin and some others climbed back into their carriages. Only Jasmin and I stayed behind.

Now we are walking along the edge of the woods behind the house at Les Sablonnières, beside a large expanse of fallow land, the site of the former estate. Without wanting to admit it and without knowing why, we are filled with anxiety. As we stroll along, we try to distract ourselves by showing each other places where hares take dust baths and little furrows in the sand that rabbits have freshly dug . . . a tightened noose . . . traces of a poacher . . . but inevitably we return to the edge of the wood from where we can see the quiet, closed house.

Below the casement window, which faces the pine trees, there is a wooden porch, covered in wild plants the wind has blown down. The glimmer of a lighted fire reflects on the windowpanes. From time to time, a shadow passes across. In the surrounding fields, in the vegetable garden, in the only farm remaining of the old dependencies, there is nothing but silence and solitude. The tenants have gone to town to celebrate their masters' good fortune.

From time to time, the wind, so full of mist that it is almost raining, moistens our faces and carries towards us the voice of a piano. Down there, in the closed-up house, someone is playing. I stop for a moment to listen. At first it is a trembling sound which, from a distance, hardly dares express its joy. It is almost like the tentative laughter of a little girl who has taken out all her toys and spread them in front of her friend. It also reminds me of the fearful joy of a woman who has put on a beautiful dress and wants to show it off, but is uncertain if it will please. This melody, which I do not know, sounds like a prayer, a supplication that fate be kind, a salutation and a genuflection to happiness.

'They are content at last,' I say to myself. 'Meaulnes is right there, next to her.'

Knowing that, being sure of it, is enough to make me completely satisfied, simple fellow that I am.

I am completely absorbed by the moment, my face as wet from the wind off the moor as if soaked by sea-spray. Then Jasmin touches my shoulder.

'Listen,' he says softly.

I look at him. He signals me not to move, and he too listens, with his head cocked, frowning.

CHAPTER VIII

FRANTZ'S CALL

'HOU-OU!'

This time, I hear it. A two-note call, high and low. I've heard it before, ages ago. Ah! I remember. It is the signal the gypsy used to hail his young companion through the railings at school. It is the call Frantz made us swear to answer, no matter where, no matter when. But what does this signify here, today?

'It's coming from the big wood of pine trees on the left,' I whisper. 'It's probably a poacher.'

Jasmin shakes his head.

'You know very well it isn't,' he said. Then, more softly, 'They've been hanging around this district since morning. At eleven o'clock I surprised Ganache on the lookout in a field near the chapel. He took off the moment he saw me. They've come some distance, perhaps by bicycle, because he was splattered in mud halfway up his back.'

'What are they looking for?'

'I've no idea. But we must chase them away without fail. We can't let them prowl around here in case all that craziness starts up again.'

I agree with him, but don't admit it.

'It would be better to join them,' I say, 'to find out what they want and make them see reason.'

Slowly, silently, bent over, we slip through the copse as far as the big pine tree from which the prolonged cry proceeds at regular intervals. It isn't actually sadder than other cries, but to both of us it sounds like a sinister omen.

It is difficult to move forward and surprise anyone in this part of the pine forest without being seen because of the spaces between the regularly planted trees. We don't even try. I place myself at one corner of the wood. Jasmin goes to the opposite corner, in order to command from outside, like me, two sides of the rectangle. If either of the gypsies tries to escape, we can shout at him. Having taken up our positions, I adopt the role of truce-maker by calling out:

'Frantz! Frantz! Don't be frightened. It's me, Seurel. I want to talk to you.'

Silence for a moment. I decide to call again, but just then from the very heart of the copse a disembodied voice commands:

'Stay where you are. He is coming to find you.'

Little by little, between the tall pines, which in the distance look tightly ranked, I distinguish the silhouette of a young man approaching us. He is covered with mud and poorly dressed. Bicycle clips secure the bottom of his trousers, and he has rammed an old cap, adorned with an anchor, on his straggly hair. Now I can see how thin he is. He appears to have been weeping.

'What do you want?' he demands in a very arrogant manner.

'And you, Frantz, what are you doing here?' I ask. 'Have you come to stir up trouble? What do you need to know? Tell me.'

This direct address makes him flush.

'I am so unhappy, so unhappy,' he finally mumbles.

Then, leaning against a tree trunk, with his head on his arm, he begins sobbing bitterly. We have taken several steps into the wood and it is perfectly silent. Even the wind is blocked by the big pine trees at the edge of the wood. But between their serried trunks, the sound of his muffled sobs rises and falls. I wait for the crisis to ease, and then I put my hand on his shoulder and say:

'Frantz, come with me. I will take you to them. They will welcome you like a lost child finally found, and everything will be all right.'

But he doesn't want to listen. In a tear-soaked voice, miserable, stubborn, and angry, he shouts:

'So Meaulnes no longer cares about me? Why doesn't he reply when I call? Why doesn't he keep his promise?'

'Listen, Frantz,' I reply, 'the time for illusions and childish pursuits is over. Don't let your mad ideas disturb the happiness of your sister and Augustin Meaulnes, both of whom you love so much.'

'But only he can save me. You know that. Only he is capable of finding the clues I am looking for. Ganache and I have scoured the whole of France for nearly three years – without result. I trusted only in your friend Meaulnes. And now he doesn't even respond when I call. Here's why. He has found his love so why can't he think about me now? He must start searching. Yvonne will let him go. She has never refused me anything.'

He shows me a face on which tears have traced dirty furrows, the face of an old, beaten-down, exhausted child. His eyes are ringed with red blotches, his chin ill-shaven, his long hair trailing over his dirty collar. With his hands in his pockets, he shivers. This is no longer the royal child dressed in glad rags, but in his heart, no doubt, he feels even more of a child than ever, imperious, capricious, and suddenly desperate. But this kind of childishness is hard to accept in someone of his age. Once he had so much youthful exuberance and pride that any mad excess seemed acceptable. But now I am tempted to complain about his lack of maturity and point out that it is time to stop playing the heady, absurd role of young romantic hero. And then I realise that our handsome Frantz of the grand passions must have been reduced to stealing in order to live, just like his companion Ganache. All that pride – to come to this!

'If I promise you,' I reply at last, after reflection, 'that in a few days Meaulnes will enter the fray again, just for you . . .'

'He will succeed, won't he? Can you be sure?' he interrupts, with his teeth chattering.

'I think so. Anything is possible with him.'

'And how will I know? Who will tell me?'

'Come back here this time next year exactly, and you will find the young woman you love.'

Promising this, I am convinced I do not have to trouble the newlyweds. I will investigate Aunt Moinel's information and set about locating the young girl myself.

The gypsy looks me in the eye with a surge of total trust. He is still fifteen years old, still and forever fifteen! The age we were at Sainte-Agathe on the evening we swept the classrooms, the evening we three swore that terrible childhood oath.

Despair overcomes him when he has to admit that they should depart. He gazes around at the woods he is about to leave once more, and I know his heart is aching.

'In three days,' he says, 'we will be travelling in Germany. We left our carriages a long way from here, and walked for thirty hours without stopping. We thought we could arrive in time to get hold of Meaulnes before the wedding and search with him for my fiancée as carefully as he sought out the domain at Les Sablonnières.'

Then, overtaken again by his terrible childishness, he says:

'Call off your friend Delouche, because if I run into him, there'll be trouble.'

I watch his grey silhouette disappear among the pines. Then I call Jasmin and we resume our watch on the little house again. Almost straight away, we spot Augustin closing the shutters, and are struck by how strange he looks.

CHAPTER IX

THE HAPPY COUPLE

LATER, I learned in detail what happened.

Once the guests had left, old Monsieur de Galais opened the door, letting the strong, moaning wind penetrate the house; then he went off towards Vieux-Nançay to lock up everything and to leave instructions at the farm. He would not return until the dinner hour. Meaulnes and his wife (whom I still call Mademoiselle de Galais) remained completely alone all afternoon in the living room at Les Sablonnières. No outdoors sound reached the young people, except for the scratching of the leafless rose branch against the windowpane. In that strong winter wind, they were like two passengers in a drifting boat, two lovers enfolded in their happiness.

'The fire is going out,' said Mademoiselle de Galais, rising to take a log from the woodbox. But Meaulnes sprang up and placed the wood on the fire himself. She reached out her hand and he took it, and they stayed there, standing in front of each other, as if they were overcome by some great news they dared not speak about.

The wind rolled with the sound of a river overflowing. From time to time, a drop of water streaked the window diagonally, the way it does on a train.

Then the girl broke away. With a mysterious smile, she opened the door into the passage and disappeared. Augustin remained alone in the half darkness for an instant. The tick-tock of a little pendulum made him remember the dining room at Sainte-Agathe. He must have thought, 'Here I am at last in the house I sought so long, whose corridors I remember being full of whispers and flittings to and fro.'

It was at that moment that he must have heard Frantz's first cry, quite close to the house. Mademoiselle de Gailais told me later that she had heard it too.

It distracted him, and as a result she had difficulty showing Meaulnes the marvellous treasures she wanted him to see: toys she played with as a little girl; photographs of her as a baby, and later in dressing-up clothes; Frantz and herself on their pretty mother's knee; and all her favourite dresses she had kept 'including the one I was wearing when you arrived in the courtyard at Saint-Agathe'. But Meaulnes could not concentrate. Nevertheless, for one brief moment, he was overwhelmed by extraordinary, unimaginable happiness.

'You're there,' he said woozily, as if just saying it made him dizzy, 'you move over to the table and your hand rests on it for a moment. When my mother was a young woman, she used to lean forward to speak to me, just the way you do. And when she sat at the piano . . .'

Mademoiselle de Galais offered to play the instrument before night fell, but it was already dark in that corner of the room and they had to light a candle. The pink lampshade added colour to her already scarlet cheeks, always a sign of great anxiety in her.

That is when, as I stood outside in the woods, I first heard her trembling song, wafted over to us by the wind, only too soon interrupted by the second cry from the two madmen, as they came towards us through the trees.

Meaulnes listened to Yvonne playing the piano for a long time, but all the while gazing silently through the window. Several times he turned towards her sweet face, so anxious and so vulnerable. Then he approached her and, very lightly, put his hand on her shoulder. She felt the light weight of a caress near her neck; she did not know how to respond.

'Night has fallen,' he said at last. 'I am going to close the shutters. But don't stop playing.'

What was going on in that dark and savage heart? I often asked myself this question, but learned the answer when it was too late. Unknown remorse? Inexplicable regret? Fear that this unexpected happiness he clung to so hard might slip through his fingers? A terrible temptation to cast away, once and for all, this marvel he had won?

He drifted outside, after one last glance at his young bride. From the edge of the woods, we could see him hesitantly close one shutter, look vaguely towards us while closing the other, and then suddenly take to his heels in our direction. We didn't have time to take cover, and he caught sight of us just as he was about to leap over a recently planted hedge that bordered a meadow. He swerved, and I noticed how distraught he was, his gaze that of a hunted animal. He prepared again to jump over the hedge beside the stream.

I cried out to him, 'Meaulnes! Augustin!' But he didn't even turn his head.

Convinced it was the only way I could restrain him, I yelled: 'Frantz is here. Wait!'

That got his attention. Gasping for air and without giving me the chance to prepare what I might say, he said:

'He's here! What does he want?'

'He's in distress,' I replied. 'He came for help finding what he's lost.'

'Ah!' said Meaulnes, lowering his head. 'That's what I thought it was. I tried in vain to suppress that thought. But where is he? Tell me quickly.'

I told him Franz had just left and it would be impossible to catch up with him now. This was a disappointment for Meaulnes. He hesitated, took two or three steps, stopped, mired in chagrin and indecision. I recounted what I had promised the young man, on his behalf, and told him about the rendezvous in a year's time at the same place.

Augustin, generally so calm, was now extraordinarily agitated and impatient.

'Ach! Why did you do that?' he asked. 'Yes, I can certainly save him, but I must do it immediately. I have to see him and speak to him. If he can forgive me, I will sort out everything. If I don't, I can no longer show my face over there.'

And he turned towards the house at Les Sablonnières.

'So,' I said, 'for a stupid childhood promise, you will destroy your happiness?'

'If it were only the promise . . .' he replied.

Thus I knew that something else bound the two young men together, but I couldn't figure out what it was.

'In any case,' I said, 'running after him won't do any good. They are now on the road to Germany.'

He was about to reply when a frantic, dishevelled figure appeared before us. It was Mademoiselle de Galais. She had been running and her face was covered in perspiration. And she must have fallen and hurt herself because she had a graze over her right eye, and blood was congealing in her hair.

It has happened to me that, while going down a street in a certain poor district in Paris, I have seen policemen intervening in a fight, in a household I had previously believed was happy, united, and honest. The disturbance had broken out all of a sudden, perhaps at the instant when the family sat down to eat, or on Sunday before an outing, or at the moment of celebrating a little boy's birthday. But now, all that is forgotten and the place is in an uproar. At the centre of the tumult, the man and woman have turned into demons, while their wailing children cling to them like limpets, imploring them to stop fighting.

Mademoiselle de Galais, when she approached Meaulnes, made me think of one of those panic-stricken children. I believe that even if all her friends, the entire village, and the whole world were watching, she would have rushed out in the same way, and would have fallen in the same way, and appeared before us dishevelled, weeping, and grimy.

But when she saw Meaulnes was still there, that he had not yet abandoned her, she placed her arm under his and laughed through her tears like a little child. They didn't say anything, but when she pulled out her handkerchief, Meaulnes took it gently from her hands. With great care, he wiped away the blood from her hair.

'We must go home now,' he said.

I watched them turn back to the house, with the strong wind of a winter evening whipping at their faces – Meaulnes, holding out his hand to help her over the rough places; Yvonne, smiling and hurrying towards the home they had abandoned for a moment.

CHAPTER X

FRANTZ'S HOUSE

I spent the whole of the following day inside the school, feeling ill at ease and not entirely reassured that the happy ending to the previous day's tumult had solved everything. Immediately after study hour, which followed the afternoon class, I took the road to Les Sablonnières. Night was falling when I arrived at the avenue of pine trees which led to the house. All the shutters were already closed. I feared that by presenting myself at this late hour on the day after a wedding, my visit might be ill-timed. So I hung around, wandering about on the boundary of the garden, always hoping to see someone coming out of the closed-up house. I hoped in vain. Even in the next-door farm, nothing moved. I had to go home, haunted by the most sombre speculations.

The next day, Saturday, I was still in the same state of uncertainty. In the evening, I snatched up my cape, my stick, and a piece of bread to eat on the way. I arrived as night was falling, only to find everything at Les Sablonnières closed up, like the day before, with a gleam of light on the first floor, but no sound, no movement. However, I noticed that this time the door to the courtyard of the farm was open, and light shone in the big kitchen. I could hear the usual sound of voices and footsteps at supper time. This reassured me without telling me much. I had nothing to say to these people, nothing to ask them. I returned to my vigil, waiting in vain, always thinking I might see the door open and Augustin's tall silhouette emerge.

It was only on Sunday, in the afternoon, that I resolved to ring the doorbell. As I made my way over the bare hillsides, I heard distant bells ringing for Sunday vespers. I felt lonely and distressed and full of dread, so I was not at all surprised when, in answer to my ring, I saw Monsieur de Galais appear alone and speak to me in a low voice: Yvonne de Galais was in bed with a high fever. Meaulnes had left on Friday morning on a long journey. No one knew when he would return.

The old man, very distressed and very sad, did not invite me in, so I took my leave right away. When the door shut, I remained on the step for a moment, my heart breaking, completely helpless, gazing at a dry wisteria branch tossing sadly in the wind, caught in a ray of sunshine.

So the secret remorse festering in Meaulnes since his stay in Paris had overcome him in the end. He had given in to it, at the expense of his own happiness.

Each Thursday and each Sunday, I went to Les Sablonnières for news of Yvonne de Galais. At last, one evening when she was still convalescing, she invited me to come in. I found her seated near the fire, in the salon whose big, low window overlooked the grounds and the woods. She was not pale, as I had expected, but still feverish, with bright red marks under her eyes, and in an extremely agitated condition. Even though she still seemed weak, she was dressed for the outdoors. She spoke little, but pronounced each sentence with extraordinary animation, as if she wished to persuade herself that her happiness had not vanished. I don't remember what we talked about, only that I asked her with hesitation when Meaulnes would return.

'I don't know when he'll return,' she replied quickly, her eyes entreating me not to ask more, so I desisted.

I returned to see her many times. We often chatted in front of the fire and in the low room where night came more quickly than anywhere else. She never talked about herself nor of her hidden pain, but she never failed to make me recount in detail the stories of student life at Sainte-Agathe.

She listened seriously, tenderly, with an almost maternal interest to the account of our adolescent misfortunes. She never seemed to be surprised, even by our most daring and dangerous childish pursuits. She had inherited a certain tender attentiveness from Monsieur de Galais, and even the memory of her brother's deplorable adventures did not weary her. The only past regret she had was, I think, that she had never been a close enough confidant for Frantz. At the moment of his collapse, he had not dared unburden himself to her, judging himself lost beyond recourse. What a heavy burden for a young woman to assume! What a dangerous task to try to help a spirit as madly fanciful as her brother's! What a daunting task to ally herself with the adventurous heart of my friend Meaulnes.

One day she showed me the most touching proof, and the most mysterious, of the faith she kept in her brother's childhood ambitions and the care she took in saving remnants of the dream–world he lived in until he was twenty years old.

It happened on an April evening as bleak as the end of autumn. For almost a month we had been enjoying a soft, premature spring, and she had started to take the kind of long walks she enjoyed, in the company of Monsieur de Galais. But that particular day, the old man was feeling tired, and I was free, so she asked me to accompany her in spite of the menacing weather. More than half a league from Les Sablonnières, while we were walking beside the pond, we were surprised by a sudden storm with rain and hail. We found shelter from the lengthy downpour in a shed, but even so the wind froze us, and we huddled together, deep in thought, gazing out at the darkening landscape. I can still see her, pale and tormented, in her sweet, prim dress.

'We ought to go back,' she said. 'We have been gone so long. Who knows what may have happened.'

But to my astonishment, when it was possible for us at last to leave our shelter, instead of going back towards Les Sablonnières, she continued on her way and asked me to follow her. After walking some distance, we arrived in front of a house I did not recognise, isolated, at the edge of a rutted road which went in the direction of Préveranges. It was a snug little cottage with a slate roof, distinguished only from the usual buildings in that part of the world by its isolation.

Judging by Yvonne de Galais's behaviour, you might have thought this house belonged to us and we were returning to it after a long trip. Bending down, she opened a little gate, and quickly and anxiously inspected the solitary place. The storm had made furrows in a large, weedy courtyard where children must have played during the long, slow afternoons at winter's end. A hoop lay soaking in a puddle. After the huge downpour, only bits of gravel remained where the children had sown flowers and peas. And finally we found a whole clutch of chicks soaked by the rain, huddled on the threshold of one of the rainsoaked doors. Almost all had died under the stiff and battered wings of their mother.

Seeing this sorry spectacle, Mademoiselle de Galais let out a stifled cry. She bent down without worrying about water or mud, sorted out the living chicks from the dead, and put the survivors in her coat pocket. She produced the key to the house, and we entered. Four doors opened on to a narrow corridor through which the wind rushed and whistled. She opened the first door on our right and made me enter a dark room where I could make out, after a stumble, a large mirror and a small bed covered with a red silk eiderdown, in the country style. After inspecting the rest of the building, she came back, carrying the chicks in a down-filled basket, which she slid carefully under the eiderdown. A languid ray of sunshine, the first and the last of the day, made our faces paler and nightfall deeper, as we stood there, frozen and worried, in the strange house.

Every so often she took a look in the nest, taking out a newly dead chick to prevent it from infecting the others. And each time it seemed as though a strong wind keened through the broken windows of the loft, sounding like the grieving of unknown children.

'This was Frantz's home when he was little,' my companion finally told me. 'He wanted a house of his own to stay in, far from everyone else, where he could go and play games whenever he pleased. My father found this fantasy so extraordinary, so funny, that he did not refuse. So, whenever it pleased Frantz, on a Thursday, a Sunday, no matter when, he used to set off and live in his house like a grown-up. The children from the nearby farms came to play with him, helped him with the housework, and worked in the garden. It was a marvellous game. When night came, he was not frightened to sleep there all by himself. We admired him so much that we didn't worry about him at all.

'The house is empty now and has been for a long time,' she continued, with a sigh. 'My father, stricken by age and sadness, hasn't made any effort to find my brother and bring him back. What could he do?

'I come here often. The peasant children nearby still come and play in the courtyard. And I like to imagine that they are Frantz's former playmates. and that he is still young and will return soon with the fiancée he has chosen.

'The children know me well. I play with them. The clutch of chicks is ours.'

It took the downpour and the incident with the chicks before she could confide in me her huge regret at having lost her brother, so mad, but so charming and so admired. I listened to her without replying, my heart full of anguish.

Once we had closed the doors and the gates and returned the chicks to the wooden coop behind the house, she took my arm sadly and I led her back home.

Weeks and months went by. Happiness vanished, became a thing of the past. Strangely enough, since Meaulnes's flight, I became the one to take the arm of the princess, the fairy queen, the mysterious love object of our adolescence. I was the one who eased her sorrow. What can I say now about our evening conversations after my classes at Saint-Benoist-des-Champs? What can I say now about the fact that, during our walks, the only subject we should have spoken about was the only one about which we remained silent? The only memory I have is this, and it has already faded: a beautiful, thin face, two eyes looking at me with eyelids slightly lowered, as if her mind were concentrated on her inner world.

I remained her faithful companion – a companion waiting with her for something we did not talk about – during a whole spring and a whole summer the likes of which we would never see again. Several times we returned during the afternoon to Frantz's house. She always opened the doors to air the place out, so that nothing would smell mouldy when the household returned. She took care of the half-wild poultry which had made themselves at home in the farmyard. And on Thursdays and Sundays, we cheered the children's games, and their screams and laughter in that solitary site made the little house seem even more empty and deserted.

CHAPTER XI

A CONVERSATION IN THE RAIN

AUGUST, vacation time, took me away from Les Sablonnières and Yvonne de Galais for my two months' holiday at Sainte-Agathe. I was back once again in the big, dry playground with its awning and the empty classrooms where I was constantly reminded of Meaulnes. Everything was filled with memories of our lost adolescence. During the long, golden days, I shut myself up in the archives and deserted classrooms, the way I did before the advent of Meaulnes. I read, I wrote, I reflected. My father was away fishing. Millie sewed or played the piano in the salon just as before. In the absolute silence of the classrooms, everything spoke of the end of the year – ripped-up paper crowns, wrapping paper from book prizes, sponged blackboards. Everything awaited autumn, the October return, and the new effort. I kept thinking that our youth was finished and we were out of luck. I marked time until my return to Les Sablonnières and the arrival of Meaulnes, even though I knew he might never reappear.

All the same, I was able to give Millie some good news when she harangued me with questions about the bride. I dreaded these questions and the seemingly innocent but very cunning manner in which she would suddenly plunge me into embarrassment, homing in on my most secret thoughts. This time I was able to pre-empt her by announcing that Meaulnes's young wife would become a mother in October.

I remember the day when Yvonne de Galais gave me this great news. Suffering from a young man's slight embarrassment, I was rendered speechless. To cover my discomfiture, I responded inconsiderately, remembering too late all the emotions I might stir up.

'You must be very happy?'

But without a moment's reflection, and without regret or remorse or bitterness, she replied with a beautiful smile:

'Yes, very happy.'

During the last week of vacation, often the most enjoyable and most romantic, a week of torrential rain, a week in which people start to light their fires, and which I normally spent hunting in the dark and dripping pines of Vieux-Nançay, I made preparations to go directly back to Saint-Benoist-des-Champs. Firmin, Aunt Julie, and my Vieux-Nançay cousins had been pestering me with questions I did not want to respond to. So I renounced the heady life of a hunter in the countryside, and went back to my schoolhouse four days before the start of classes.

I arrived before night in the courtyard, already carpeted with yellow autumn leaves. After the coachman left, I went sadly into the echoing, closed-up dining room and unpacked the provisions my mother had given me. After a light meal, eaten half-heartedly because of impatience and anxiety, I put on my cape and walked feverishly towards to the outskirts of Les Sablonnières.

I didn't want to be intrusive by bursting in the very day I arrived home. However, I was bolder than I was in February. After I had circled the property, where the only light shone from her window, I went through the garden gate and sat down on a bench next to the hedge in the fading light, happy simply to be there, near the source of what thrilled and disturbed me more than anything in the world.

It grew darker and darker and a fine rain began to fall. With my head lowered, I stared at my shoes, unaware they were gradually filling with water. Darkness and chill slowly enveloped me but this did not interrupt my reverie. I thought nostalgically about the way the muddy paths of Sainte-Agathe would look on this September evening. I imagined the mist-filled square, the butcher's son whistling as he went to the well, the bright lights of the café, and a joyous coachload of people with a carapace of open umbrellas arriving at Uncle Florentin's just before the end of the holidays. I said to myself sadly: 'What is the point of all this happiness since Meaulnes cannot be here to share it with me and his bride?'

I lifted my head and saw her just a few steps in front of me. Her shoes had made a light sound on the sandy path, which I had taken to be water dripping off the hedge. She wore a long, black, wool wrap on her head and shoulders, and the fine rain looked like powder on her forehead and hair. She must have seen me from the bedroom window which overlooked the garden. She kept coming towards me. It reminded me of the way my mother worried about my being outside at night when I was a child. Millie would look for me, intending to say, 'You must come inside,' but finding that a stroll in the rain at night was quite delightful, she merely said, 'You'll catch cold,' and remained outdoors herself, chatting with me for a long time.

Yvonne de Galais held out her hand, and it was hot to the touch. Abandoning the idea of making me go inside, she sat down on the dryer end of the lichen-covered bench, while I stood, with one knee on it, leaning towards her so that I could hear.

First she scolded me, but in a friendly way, for having cut short my vacation.

'I had to, so that I could keep you company sooner,' I replied.

'It's true,' she said with a quiet sigh. 'I am still alone. Augustin has not come back yet.'

Taking this sigh to mean sadness and a stifled reproach, I began slowly:

'He has so much folly in such a noble head! Perhaps his love of adventure is stronger than anything.'

She interrupted me, and there that very evening, she talked to me about Meaulnes for the first and last time.

'François Seurel, my friend, don't talk like that,' she said softly. 'Only we – only I am guilty. Think about what we have done. We told him, "Here is happiness. Here is what you have looked for all your childhood. Here is the bride, the fulfilment of your dreams!"

'We trapped him. He couldn't help being gripped first by hesitation, then by fear, then by terror. He couldn't help giving in to the desire to flee.'

'Yvonne,' I said quietly, 'you know well that you were his true happiness.'

'How could I for an instant think such a conceited thought? That thought is the root of all our trouble. I once said to you, "Perhaps I can do nothing more for him." But in my heart, I was thinking, "Since he looked for me so hard, and since I love him so much, I must be able to make him happy." But when I saw him beside me, overcome with feverishness, anxiety, and that mysterious remorse of his, I understood that I was just another feeble woman.

'"I am not worthy of you," he kept repeating at dawn after our wedding night.

'I tried to console and reassure him, but nothing soothed his anguish. Then I said: "If you must leave, if I have come into your life at the very moment when nothing makes you happy, if you must leave me for a while so that you can return peacefully, I beg you to go."'

In the dark, I could make out that her eyes were raised to me. It felt as though she had made her confession and was waiting anxiously for my approval or condemnation. What could I say? I kept thinking of Meaulnes as he used to be, gauche and savage, always accepting punishment rather than making excuses or asking for the permission he would certainly have been granted. Yvonne de Galais should have been harsher with him, should have taken his head between her hands and said, 'What does it matter what you have done? I love you. All men are sinners.' Because of her generosity and her willingness to sacrifice her happiness, she had made the mistake of sending him off on his adventure again. But how could I disapprove of so much kindness, so much love?

Troubled to the bottom of our hearts, we listened in silence to the cold rain dripping on the hedges and from the tree branches.

'So he left in the morning,' she continued. 'But in future, nothing will part us. He kissed me simply, the way a husband kisses his young wife before leaving on a long journey.'

She rose. I took her feverish hand in mind, then her arm, as we walked up the dark avenue.

'Has he ever written to you?' I asked.

'Never,' she replied.

Then we both began to reflect on the adventurous life he was leading at that moment in France or Germany, and spoke of him in a way we had never done before. Forgotten details, old impressions returned to our memories while we slowly approached the house, and we paused with each step so as not to leave anything out. I listened to that precious low voice as we wandered around the garden and, filled with my old enthusiasm, I spoke affectionately, without flagging, about the one who had abandoned both of us.

CHAPTER XII

THE BURDEN

CLASSES were due to start on Monday. On Saturday evening, at about five o'clock, a woman from the domain came into the schoolyard where I was busy sawing wood for the winter. She announced that a little girl had been born at Les Sablonnières. The birth had been difficult; they summoned the midwife from Préveranges at nine o'clock in the evening; at midnight, they hitched up the coach again to fetch the doctor from Vierzon. He had to use forceps. The baby's head was injured and she cried a great deal, but she seemed to be thriving. Yvonne de Galais had endured her labour with extraordinary bravery, but was now very weak.

Pleased on the whole with the news, I left my work, ran to get a coat, and followed the woman back to Les Sablonnières. Cautiously, in case either mother or child were asleep, I climbed the narrow wooden staircase leading to the upper floor. Monsieur de Galais, looking tired but happy, invited me into the room where the curtained cradle had been located for the time being.

I had never before entered a house where a baby had been born that very day. How strange and mysterious and beneficent! It was such a beautiful evening – a true summer's evening – and Monsieur de Galais did not hesitate to open the window overlooking the courtyard. He leaned against the casement near me, and described the night's drama with a mixture of exhaustion and elation. Listening to him, I was vaguely aware of the new occupant of the room.

Behind the curtains, she began to cry, a tiny, prolonged wail. Monsieur de Galais said softly:

'It's the head injury that makes her cry.'

Automatically, he began rocking the little curtained package, and I had the feeling he had been doing this since morning and it had become a habit.

'She's already laughed,' he said, 'and she'll take your finger. But, wait, you still haven't seen her!'

He drew aside the curtain and I looked at a tiny, red, swollen face, its little cranium misshapen by the forceps.

'It's nothing,' said Monsieur de Galais. 'The doctor says that everything will heal by itself. Give her your hand. She will grip it.'

I discovered a world I had never known, and felt my heart swelling with joy.

Monsieur de Galais gently opened the door into his daughter's room. She was not asleep.

'You can go in,' he said.

She was stretched out on the bed, her blonde hair spread around her feverish face. She held out her hand and smiled wearily while I complimented her on her daughter. In a rather hoarse voice, and with unaccustomed toughness – the toughness of someone returning from a fight – she said with a smile: 'Yes, but they damaged her.'

Then I had to leave so as not to tire her.

In the afternoon of the next day, Sunday, I was almost joyful as I hurried to Les Sablonnières, but a sign pinned to the door stopped me in my tracks:

Please do not ring

I couldn't imagine what it meant. I knocked quite loudly. From inside I heard muffled steps, running. Someone I did not know opened the door. It turned out to be the doctor from Vierzon.

'What's going on?' I asked sharply.

'Shhh, shhh,' he replied in a quiet, angry voice. 'The little girl almost died last night. And the mother is very ill.'

Dismayed, I followed the doctor upstairs, hard on his heels. The baby was sleeping in her cradle, but she looked almost dead because she was so pale, so white. The doctor thought he could still save her. As for the mother, he could promise nothing. He gave me long explanations, as if I was the sole family friend. He spoke about pulmonary congestion, of an embolism. He hesitated, he was unsure. Then Monsieur de Galais came in, haggard and trembling, dreadfully aged in two days.

He led me into her room scarcely knowing what he was doing.

'Yvonne must not be frightened,' he said to me softly. 'The doctor insists we persuade her all is well.'

Like the previous evening, she was stretched out with her head tilted back. All the blood had gone to her face. Her cheeks and her forehead were flaming red and her eyes rolled up as if she were choking. Yvonne de Galais held death at bay with inexpressible courage and sweetness.

She could not speak, but held out her burning hand to me in a gesture of so much loving friendship that I almost burst out sobbing.

'Well, well,' said Monsieur de Galais loudly with a dreadful sort of mad playfulness, 'you can see she doesn't look too bad.'

I didn't know how to reply, but I kept her hand in mine, the horribly hot hand of a young woman who was dying.

She tried to tell me something or to ask me something – I don't know which. Her eyes turned towards me, then towards the window, as though she wanted me to go outside and look for someone. But then she was seized by a terrible spasm of choking. Her beautiful blue eyes which had just appealed to me so tragically, rolled back in her head. Her cheeks and forehead darkened as she struggled to suppress her terror and despair. The doctor and the women all rushed to her side with an oxygen bottle, napkins, flasks. Bending over her, Monsieur de Galais cried out in a desperate, trembling voice as though she were already far away:

'Don't be frightened, Yvonne. It's nothing. You don't need to be frightened!'

Then the crisis passed. She could breathe again but continued to choke from time to time; her eyes went blank and her head tilted back as she struggled, incapable of looking at me and speaking to me even for an instant, incapable of rising out of the abyss into which she had already sunk.

As I could be of no use, I decided to leave, even though I could certainly have stayed a little while longer; and I am seized with regret at this thought. Why did I leave so soon? Because I was still hopeful. I had persuaded myself that her death was not imminent.

Arriving at the border of pine trees behind the house, remembering her look as she turned towards the window, I peered, with the care of a sentinel or someone on a manhunt, into the depths of the wood through which Augustin had arrived and where he had fled the previous winter. Alas! Nothing moved. Not even the suspicion of a shadow or swaying branch, but soon enough from the direction of Préveranges, I heard the tinkling of a little bell. A child appeared at the turn in the road, wearing a red skull cap and schoolboy smock, followed by a priest. I left, gulping back my tears.

Classes started the next day. By seven o'clock, two or three lads had already appeared in the schoolyard. I hesitated for a long time before going down and making my presence felt. When I finally appeared, I turned the key in the lock of the classroom which had been shut up for two months and smelled of mould. Then, what I dreaded most in the world happened. I watched the biggest schoolboy detach himself from the group playing under the awning and approach me with the news that 'the young lady at Les Sablonnières' had died the previous evening, at nightfall.

Everything becomes jumbled, everything is confounded by my grief. I feel as though I will never have the courage to start classes again. Just crossing the dry schoolyard is enough to exhaust me. Everything hurts, everything tastes bitter because she has died. The world is empty. The holidays, finished. The long coach journeys, finished. The mysterious celebration, finished. Nothing but sorrow remains.

I told the children there would be no classes this morning, and they left in groups to spread the news around. I donned my black hat and a jacket bordered with braid, and set off miserably towards Les Sablonnières.

Here I am, in front of the house we searched for so often during three long years! It is in this house that Yvonne de Galais, wife of Augustin Meaulnes, died yesterday evening. A stranger could take the house for a chapel, so deep is the silence in this desolated spot.

All we are left with on this fine morning at the start of the school year is the perfidious autumn sun, sliding under the branches. How can I struggle against this frightful outrage, this choking surge of tears? We had found Yvonne de Galais, and we had won her heart. She was my companion's wife, and I loved her too with a deep and secret love I never revealed. I had only to look at her to be as happy as a child. If one day I wanted to marry another young woman, and if Yvonne had lived, she would have been the first person to hear my great news.

Yesterday's note remains near the bell beside the door. The coffin has already been carried into the vestibule on the ground floor. The baby's nurse meets me on the first floor, and tells me about Yvonne's end as she gently opens the door.

There she lies. No more fever, no more struggle. No more redness, no more waiting. Nothing but silence, and a stiff, insensible, white face surrounded by cotton wool, a dead brow above which her thick and lifeless hair springs.

Monsieur de Galais, crouched in a corner, has his back turned to us. In his stockinged feet, he rummages with terrible insistence in the disordered drawers he has pulled out of an armoire. From time to time, he takes out an old photograph, already yellowing, of his daughter, and sobs so hard that his shoulders shake, as though he is laughing.

The burial is set for noon. The doctor fears the rapid decomposition which sometimes follows an embolism. This is why her face, and in fact her whole body, is surrounded by cotton wool soaked in phenol.

She is dressed in a wonderful dark blue velvet garment, embroidered here and there with silver stars; someone has had to iron its old-fashioned, leg-of-lamb sleeves. When the men try to bring the coffin upstairs, they find it impossible to make the turn. Someone suggests hauling it up by a rope through the window from outside, and letting it down again the same way. But Monsieur de Galais, still burrowing through a pile of memories, intervenes with astonishing vehemence.

'It would be far better,' he says in a voice shaky with tears and anger, 'far better than trying such a terrible thing, if I were to carry her downstairs in my arms.'

And the poor, weak man insists on doing just that, at the risk of falling halfway down and rolling to the bottom with her!

I move forward, taking the only course of action open to me. With the help of the doctor and a woman, I pass one arm under the stretched-out body, the other under her legs, and lift her up against my chest. Supported by my left arm, her shoulders leaning against my right arm, her fallen head resting against my chin, she is a terrible weight on my heart. Step by slow step, I descend the long, narrow staircase. Downstairs everything is ready.

My arms burn with fatigue. With her weight on my chest, I lose breath with each step. I hang on to the heavy, lifeless body, and lower my head on to her head. I breathe laboriously, and inhale her blonde hair into my mouth – dead hair which tastes of the earth. This taste of earth and death, this weight on my heart, are all that remain of the great adventure, and of you, Yvonne de Galais, so eagerly pursued, so dearly loved.

CHAPTER XIII

THE MONTHLY WORKBOOK

IN that house of sad memories, where women rocked and consoled a tiny, ailing baby all day, it was not long before old Monsieur de Galais took to his bed. During the first severe cold snap of winter, he slipped peacefully away from this life. I could not hold back my tears at the bedside of this charming old man, whose indulgence, combined with his son's fantasies, had been the cause of our whole adventure. Fortunately, he died completely unaware of all that had happened, and in almost total silence. He had no relatives or friends in this region of France, so he made me the sole legatee of his will until Meaulnes's return. I would account for everything to Meaulnes – if he ever showed up.

I lived at Les Sablonnières from then on. I only went to Saint-Benoist to teach, leaving early in the morning, lunching at noon on a meal prepared at the domain and reheated on the school stove. I returned in the evening as soon as possible after study hour. In this way I stayed close to the child, whom the farm women took care of. And above all, I improved my chances of encountering Augustin, should he appear at Les Sablonnières one day.

Besides I never gave up hope of coming across something in the house, in the furniture, in the drawers, that would reveal how he passed his time during the long silence of the preceeding years – and perhaps thus be able to grasp the reasons for his flight, or at least to find some trace of him. I had already inspected I don't know how many cupboards and desks in vain, opened a large number of ancient boxes of all shapes in the box room, some filled with bundles of old letters and yellowing photographs of the de Galais family, others crammed with artificial flowers and old-fashioned feather decorations. These boxes exuded an odour, a faint perfume which, for an entire day, reawoke such memories and regrets that I had to stop my research.

At last, in the attic, on one of my days off, I caught sight of a small trunk. It looked old and was long and low, made of pigskin, and had been gnawed on. I realised that it was Augustin's school trunk, and kicked myself for not having started my research right there. I was able to spring the rusty lock quite easily. The trunk was crammed with books and notebooks from Sainte-Agathe. Arithmetic, literature, books of tests, everything! With tenderness rather than curiosity, I began to go through it all, rereading dictations we had copied so often that I knew them by heart: 'The Aqueduct' by Rousseau, 'An Adventure in Calabria' by P.-L. Courier, 'Letter from George Sand to her Son'.

I also found a monthly workbook. I was surprised because these workbooks belonged to the school, and students were not allowed to remove them. It was green with yellowing edges, and the student's name, *Augustin Meaulnes*, was written on the cover in wonderful, round handwriting. I opened it. From the date of the homework, April 189 . . . I recognised that Meaulnes had started writing in it a few days before leaving Sainte-Agathe. The first pages were executed with almost religious care, which was the rule when we worked in our composition books. But he had only written three pages. The next few pages were blank, and this was why Meaulnes had taken it.

Kneeling on the ground, reflecting on the rules and regulations which filled up so much of our adolescence, I flicked through the empty pages, and that is how I discovered more writing. After leaving four pages blank, the writing started again.

It was still Meaulnes's handwriting, but scribbled and scarcely legible. Brief, uneven paragraphs were separated by skipped lines. Sometimes an incomplete sentence. Sometimes a date. From the first line, I reckoned it might contain information about Meaulnes's life in Paris, clues to the trail I was looking for. I went downstairs into the dining room to skim through this strange document at my leisure, by the light of day.

It was a capricious winter's day. Sometimes bright sunshine threw shadow squares from the windows on to the white curtains; at other times, the sharp wind flung a burst of hail onto the windowpanes. In front of the window near the fire, I read the following lines which explained so much. Here is an exact copy.

CHAPTER XIV

THE SECRET

I passed under her window once again. The panes were still dusty, made even more opaque by the double curtains behind them. If Yvonne de Galais were to open the window, I would have nothing to say to her now that she is married. What can I do? How can I go on living?

Saturday, 13 February. On the quay, I re-encountered the young girl I met last June while waiting in front of the closed-up house, the one who had given me information. I spoke to her, and as we walked along, I glanced sideways at the slight defects in her face: a little wrinkle at the corner of her mouth, slightly hollow cheeks, and powder accumulated at the edge of her nostrils. She turned to me suddenly and looked me straight in the face, perhaps because she was more beautiful full face than in profile, and spoke briefly.

'You amuse me, and you remind me of a young man who courted me some time ago in Bourges. He was actually my fiancé.'

Later on, when the gas-lamps were lit and reflecting their light on the wet pavement, she suddenly drew near to me and asked to be taken to the theatre that evening with her sister. I noticed for the first time that she was dressed in mourning, wore a hat more suitable for an older woman, and carried a handsome umbrella, as slim as a cane. Because I was standing close to her my nails caught on the crepe of her bodice when I gesticulated. I was reluctant to grant her request. She was angry and wanted to leave immediately.

Then I had to coax her to stay. A workman passing by in the dark joked in an undertone:

'Don't go with him, little one. He'll get you in trouble!!'

And we stood there, both of us dumbfounded.

At the theatre. The two young women, my friend, whose name is Valentine Blondeau, and her sister, arrived covered by thin shawls. Valentine was seated in front of me, and kept turning around anxiously, as if trying to work out what I wanted from her. I felt almost happy being close to her, and responded each time with a smile.

We were surrounded by women in low-cut dresses, and we joked about this. At first she smiled, but then said: 'I mustn't laugh at them. My dress is very revealing too.' And she wrapped herself up in her shawl. Indeed, I had noticed that in her haste to change her outfit, she had turned back the top of her high-necked blouse under the square of black lace.

There is something wretched and infantile about her that I can't quite put my finger on, something in her gaze both pathetic and daring that attracts me. When I am with her, I never cease to think about my strange adventure because she is the only person in the world who has given me information about the people at the domain. I wanted to question her again about the house on the boulevard, but she pre-empted me with such embarrassing questions that I couldn't reply. I think we'll be mute on the subject of Les Sablonnières from now on.

But I know I will see her again. Why? What good will it do? Am I now condemned for ever to follow the tracks of anyone emitting the slightest whiff of my wasted opportunity at the domain?

At midnight, alone in the deserted street, I asked myself what this new twist meant for me. I walked alongside houses like rows of cardboard boxes in which a whole army of people was sleeping. I was tired. I was hungry. Instead of dining, I too had hurried to change my clothes for the theatre. When I reached my room, I remained seated on the edge of the bed for a long time before I lay down, feeling nervous and jittery, in the grips of a vague remorse. Why?

I suddenly remembered a decision taken a month or so ago: I had resolved to creep around to the back of the house in the dead of night, towards one o'clock, to open the garden gate, to enter like a thief, and to look for any clue whatsover that would permit me to find the lost domain, so that I could see Yvonne again, just see her.

I must record that the sisters never wanted me to take them home nor tell me where they lived. But I followed them for as long as I could, and I learned that they lived on a little, winding street in the vicinity of Notre-Dame. But what was the number of the house? I guessed that they were dressmakers or milliners.

Without telling her sister, Valentine made a rendezvous with me for Thursday at four o'clock in front of the same theatre.

'If I am not there on Thursday,' she said, 'come back on Friday at the same time, then Saturday, and so on, every day.'

Thursday, 18 February. I left to meet her in a strong wind heavy with clouds, and was sure it was about to pour with rain.

I walked along the semi-dark streets with a heavy heart. A drop of water fell on me. I was afraid that a downpour would prevent her from coming. But the wind picked up again and the rain held off. High in the grey afternoon sky – sometimes grey and sometimes brilliant – the wind played with a huge cloud. And there I was, trapped on the ground, in for a miserable wait.

In front of the theatre. By the end of fifteen minutes, I was convinced that she would not come. From the embankment where I stood to catch a distant view of her crossing the bridge by which she would approach, I watched processions of people passing over. I scrutinised all the young women in mourning walking in my direction. I felt myself almost grateful to those who resembled her until they were close up because they gave me hope for a while.

An hour's wait. I was weary. At nightfall, a policeman dragged a hooligan, spitting out every filthy curse he knew, to the neighbourhood police station. The policeman was furious, pale and speechless. In the entry, he began to hit the boy, and then shut the door to prying eyes so that he could beat the wretched fellow in peace. A terrible thought came to me – I had renouced paradise and was trudging towards the gates of hell.

Tired of waiting, I left and made my way to a narrow street between the Seine and Notre-Dame, which I knew was not far from their house. All alone, I walked up and down. From time to time, a maid or a housewife scuttled out into the drizzle to do a bit of shopping before nightfall. But nothing of interest happened, and I left. The sun through the rain seemed to be holding back the night as I passed the place where we had planned to meet. More of a crowd than before – a black swarm . . .

Suppositions. Despair. Fatigue. I hung on to this thought: tomorrow. Tomorrow, at the same time and place, I would go back and wait for her. I couldn't wait for tomorrow to arrive. I was bored by the thought of the evening yawning ahead of me and tomorrow morning's idle passage of time. But wasn't today nearly finished? Once I was back home, I sat by the fire and listened to the newsboys hawking the evening papers. Undoubtedly, in her house somewhere in the city near Notre-Dame, she heard them too.

She: Valentine.

I wanted to conjure away the evening that weighed on me so heavily. As the minutes crept by, I thought about other people who had placed their hopes, their love, and their ebbing strength in this day. Some were dying, and some awaiting a reckoning, wishing day would never come. There were others for whom tomorrow would bring remorse, and still others who were exhausted, for whom this night would never be long enough to provide the rest they needed. And I who had squandered this day, what right did I have to summon up tomorrow?

Friday evening. I thought I would be writing: 'Again, I did not see her.' And everything would be over.

But, when I arrived at the theatre at four o'clock, there she was, slim and serious, dressed in black, with a little powder on her face. She had a ruff around her neck which, combined with her sad but mischievious air, made her resemble a pierrot with a guilty secret. She had come to tell me that she wished to part immediately, and she would not come back again.

However, at nightfall, there we still were, walking slowly side by side, along a gravel path at the Tuileries. She told me her story but in such a shrouded way that I could barely understand her. She referred to 'my lover' when she talked about the fiancé she did not marry, and I think she did it on purpose, to shock me and prevent me from becoming attached to her.

It irks me to write down what she said:

'Do not trust me.'

'My life has been one silly mistake after another.'

'I have run through the streets alone.'

'I drove my fiancé to despair. I left him because he admired me too much. I was a creature of his imagination. He had no idea what I was really like. I am full of faults. We would have been very unhappy.'

I kept catching her out at making herself seem worse than she was. I think she wanted to prove she was justified in the silly behaviour she had mentioned, that she had nothing to regret, and was unworthy of the happiness that had been offered to her.

Another time, she studied my face and said, 'What I like about you, I don't know why, is that you make me remember . . . '

Another time, she said, 'I still love him more than you think.'

And once she exclaimed suddenly, sharply, brutally, sadly, 'What do you want? Do you love me, you too? Do you plan to ask for my hand, you too?'

I stammered. I don't know how I replied. Perhaps I said, 'Yes.'

This rudimentary journal stopped there. A muddle of illegible, shapeless, crossed-out drafts of letters followed.

What a shaky engagement it must have been! Valentine stopped working at Meaulnes's request, and he occupied himself with preparations for their wedding. But he must have disappeared several times, still in thrall to the desire to keep searching, to set off again on the trail of his lost love. In these tragic, confused letters, he sought to justify himself to Valentine.

CHAPTER XV

THE SECRET, PART II

THEN the journal started up again. He noted some memories from a trip they made together to the countryside, but I don't know where. Here's something strange: from that moment on, perhaps because of propriety, the journal was composed in a manner so cut up, so formless, and scribbled down so hurriedly that I've had to gather up the bits and reconstruct this part of his story from them.

14 June. When he woke early in the morning in his room at the inn, the sun was lighting up the red design on the dark curtain. Farm workers in the room below were talking loudly as they drank their morning coffee, crudely but calmly expressing annoyance with one of their bosses. Meaulnes would have heard this buzz of conversation through his sleep. He paid no attention at first. Everything melded together into one impression of the country at the delicous beginning of the long vacation: the curtain, reddened by the sun, scattered with a design of bunches of grapes, and the morning voices floating up to the silent bedroom.

He rose, knocked gently on the adjoining door without getting a reply, and opened it without a sound. He gazed at Valentine and understood where all this peaceful happiness had come from. She was sleeping silently, absolutely still; her breathing was as quiet as a bird's. He spent a long time looking at her childlike face, her closed eyes. She slept so peacefully that he did not want to wake her, and never to trouble her.

The only movement to show she was no longer asleep was when her eyes opened and she looked at him.

Meaulnes returned to her room after she was dressed.

'We're late,' she said, and suddenly took on the role of housewife, tidying the rooms, and brushing the outfit Meaulnes had worn the previous evening. But when she started on his trousers, she became upset because they were covered in thick mud. She hesitated, and then took up a knife and with great care scraped off the first layer of mud before brushing them.

'That is what the boys of Sainte-Agathe did when they fell in the mud,' said Meaulnes.

'My mother taught me the trick,' said Valentine.

This was the perfect companion for a hunter and peasant like Meaulnes – before his mysterious adventure.

15 June. To their annoyance, they were invited to dinner at the farm, thanks to some friends who introduced them as man and wife. Valentine behaved as shyly as a newly-wed.

The table was covered with a white cloth, and candles had been lit in the candelabra at either end, like at a peaceful country wedding. Faces as they bent towards the faint candlelight were bathed in shadow.

Valentine sat to the right of Patrice (the farmer's son), with Meaulnes next to her; he was taciturn throughout the meal, even though almost all the conversation was directed towards him. His resolution to pretend, in this distant village, that Valentine was his wife, in order to avoid awkward comments, was making him feel guilty. And while Patrice directed the dinner in the manner of a country gentleman, Meaulnes kept thinking, 'It is I who should be presiding over my own wedding feast this evening, in a low room like this one, a beautiful room I remember so well . . .'

Beside him, Valentine timidly refused everything she was served. She might have been taken for a peasant girl. With each offering, she looked at Meaulnes, seeking refuge. Patrice persisted in trying to make her empty her glass, and eventually Meaulnes leaned towards her and said softly:

'You must drink, my little Valentine.'

Then she drank obediently, and Patrice smilingly congratulated Meaulnes for having a wife who obeyed so well.

But both Valentine and Meaulnes remained silent and thoughtful. They were exhausted, and their feet, which had been soaked in mud as they walked, now froze on the cold kitchen tiles. And from time to time, Meaulnes was obliged to refer to Valentine as his wife:

'My wife Valentine, my wife . . .'

Each time he softly pronounced this word in front of these unknown countryfolk, he felt he was committing a sin.

17 June. The afternoon of this last day began badly.

Patrice and his wife accompanied them on their walk, but as they proceeded down the uneven, heather-covered slope, the two couples became separated. Meaulnes and Valentine sat down among the junipers in a little copse.

The wind carried with it drops of rain and the weather deteriorated. The afternoon developed a bitter taste, a taste of such tedium that even love itself could not dissipate it.

They stayed for a long time in their hiding place, sheltered under the branches, speaking little. Then the weather cleared, and they believed all would go well from then on.

They began to speak of love. Valentine, in particular, talked and talked.

'This is what my fiancé promised me. What a child he was! Right away we would have a house, a cottage deep in the countryside. It would be completely ready, he said. We would arrive there at nightfall on our wedding night, as though we were returning from a long journey. And along the roads, in the courtyard, hidden in the woods, unseen children would celebrate us, singing out, "Long live the bride." Such crazy fantasies!'

Taken aback, Meaulnes listened carefully, hearing in all this an echo of something he already knew. Valentine's voice was tinged with regret as she recounted her story, but she was frightened she might have wounded him, and turned towards him with a rush of affection and sweetness.

'I want to give you everything I have, even my most precious possession, but you must burn it!'

Looking at him fixedly, anxiously, she pulled a small packet of her fiancé's letters out of her pocket, and held it out to him.

Meaulnes immediately recognised the fine handwriting. Why on earth hadn't he thought of this before? The writing was that of Frantz the gypsy; he had seen it once before, on the desperate note left in the bedroom at the domain.

They were now walking down a narrow path, among daisies and tall grass, obliquely lit by the five o'clock sun. So great was Meaulnes's astonishment that he couldn't immediately understand what a change in direction this signified for him. He read the letters because she asked him to read them. Childish sentences, sentimental, pathetic. Here's an example from the last letter:

'*So you have lost the little heart, my sweet, unforgivable Valentine. What will happen to us now? I am not superstitious, but . . .*'

Meaulnes read, half blinded by regret and anger, his face rigid, pale, his eyes twitching. Seeing him like this, Valentine was worried; she looked at what he was reading, and then she became upset too.

'It was a jewel he gave me,' she explained rapidly, 'and he made me swear to keep it safe for ever. Just one of his crazy ideas.'

But this exasperated Meaulnes even more.

'Crazy!' he said, putting the letters in his pocket. 'Why do you keep repeating this word? Why did you never want to believe in him? I knew him. He was the most marvellous boy in the world.'

'You knew Frantz de Galais?!' she exclaimed, overcome with emotion.

'He was my best friend. He was my brother in adventure. And now I have taken his fiancée!

'You did such harm,' he continued furiously, 'you who never

believed in anything. You are the cause of it all. Thanks to you we've lost everything. Lost everything!'

She tried to speak, to take his hand, but he pushed her away roughly.

'Go away. Leave me.'

'If that's . . . what you want,' she stammered half-crying, her face aflame, 'I will return to Bourges with my sister. But if you do not come and take me away, my father will be too poor to keep me there, as you well know. So I will set off again for Paris to wander the streets the way I did once before. And because you made me give up my profession, I am bound to become a fallen woman . . .'

She ran to fetch her belongings, and set off for the train while Meaulnes, without saying goodbye, continued walking along aimlessly.

Another break in the entries.

Then followed drafts of letters, the letters of a man unable to make a decision, a man astray. On his return to La Ferté-d'Angillon, he wrote to Valentine, apparently affirming his resolution never to see her again and giving precise reasons for this but, in reality, probably hoping for a reply. In one of these letters, he asked her what, in his confusion, he had not thought of asking before: did she know where to find the domain? In another letter, he begged her to reconcile with Frantz de Galais, and vowed he would take it upon himself to find him. All these letters, of which I saw the drafts, can't have been sent. But he must have sent two or three without ever obtaining a reply. This was a period of terrible, miserable conflict for him, spent in total isolation. But since the chance of ever seeing Yvonne de Galais was out of the question, he must have felt his resolve weakening. From the pages that follow – the last in his journal – I assume that, one fine morning at the beginning of the holidays, he must have hired a bicycle to go to Bourges and visit the cathedral.

He left very early in the morning, and cycled along the beautiful, straight road through the woods, dreaming up a thousand ways of presenting himself in a dignified way, but without asking for a reconciliation, to the woman he had driven away.

I have patched together the last four pages, and they recount this journey and this last mistake.

CHAPTER XVI

THE SECRET (END)

25 August. After searching for a long time, Meaulnes found Valentine Blondeau's house on the other side of Bourges, out in the new suburbs. A woman – Valentine's mother – was standing on the doorstep, as though expecting his arrival. A fine figure of a housewife, rumpled and heavy, but still beautiful, she watched with curiosity as he came towards her. When he asked if the Misses Blondeau were at home, she explained kindly that they had been in Paris since the fifteenth of the month.

'They made me promise not to tell anyone where they were going,' she added, 'but letters to their previous address will be forwarded.'

As he pushed his bicycle back across the small garden, he intoned to himself:

'She has gone. Everything is finished the way I decreed. She warned me, "Without doubt, I will become a fallen woman." I have driven her to this. I cast her out. Frantz's fiancée is lost because of me!'

He kept muttering, 'So much the better! So much the better!' while knowing that, on the contrary, it was actually, 'So much the worse', and he was convinced that under this woman's eyes he would stumble and fall to his knees before reaching the gate.

He didn't feel like lunch, but stopped anyway in a café where he wrote at length to Valentine, giving voice to the desperate cry that kept rising up and choking him. His letter repeated endlessly, 'How could you do this? How *could* you do this? How could you resign yourself to a life like that? How could you throw yourself away?'

Some officers sat nearby, drinking. One of them loudly recounted his experience with a certain woman, and Meaulnes caught snatches of the conversation. 'I told her . . . You know me well . . . I spend time with your husband every evening!' The others laughed and turned their heads aside to spit behind the benches. Gaunt and dusty as a beggar, Meaulnes looked at them and imagined them dandling Valentine on their knees. He rode his bicycle around and around the cathedral, mumbling to himself that 'after all, the cathedral is the real reason I came here'. Visible at the end of all roads leading to the deserted square, the building rose up, enormous and indifferent. The narrow, dirty streets resembled alleys around village churches. Here and there, he saw a red light advertising a house of ill repute, and felt his grief returning in this dirty, depraved, quarter, sheltered as in times past by the cathedral's flying buttresses. A peasant's fear overcame him and a revulsion against this city church surrounded by dens of inquity. Its niches were carved with all the vices, and it could offer him no remedy for the pure agony of love.

Two girls walked past, their arms around each other's waists, and stared at him brazenly. Out of disgust or in jest, to somehow avenge his love or to wreck it, Meaulnes followed them slowly on his bicycle. One of them, a wretched creature with thin, blonde hair pulled back by a false chignon, set up a rendezvous with him for six o'clock in the Archbishop's garden, the very garden where Frantz, in one of his letters, had set up a rendezvous with poor Valentine.

Meaulnes didn't refuse, knowing he would have left the town long before then. She kept waving vaguely at him from her low window on the sloping street until he disappeared.

He was in a hurry to be off, but before leaving could not resist the gloomy idea of going past Valentine's house one last time. He sized it up and added it to his stock of sadness. It was one of the last houses in the city's outskirts, after which the street became a country road.

Opposite the house lay a square of vacant ground. There was no one anywhere – no faces peered out of the windows, no one was visible in the courtyard. A single, dirty girl with powder all over her face walked by, two ragged urchins trailing behind her.

This was the house where Valentine had spent her childhood, where she first saw the world through her sensible, confident eyes. Later, she had worked behind these windows, sewing. And Frantz had come to see her, to smile at her, in this suburban street. But nothing was left, nothing at all. The dreary evening dragged on and Meaulnes kept imagining that Valentine, lost somewhere or another, was remembering this dismal place at the same moment, this place to which she would never return.

The long journey ahead provided a last bulwark, a last forced distraction before he was completely engulfed by sorrow.

He set off. Along the roadside, in the valley, between the trees, at the water's edge, delightful farm houses revealed pointed gables decorated with green lattice. Without doubt, over there, on the lawns, young girls were talking in minute detail about love. He imagined their souls, their beautiful souls.

But for Meaulnes at that moment, only one love existed, an unsatisfied love, a love he had cruelly slapped down. The young woman he should have protected above all others was the very one he had sent to her ruin.

Several hasty lines in the journal told me he had decided to find Valentine again at any cost before it was too late. A date on the corner of a page made me realise that Madame Meaulnes was preparing his clothes for precisely that journey when I arrived in La Ferté-d'Angillon and upset everything. In the abandoned town hall on a beautiful morning at the end of August, Meaulnes had been jotting down his memories and his plans when I pushed open the door and brought him the news he had given up hope of hearing. He had been trapped again, stopped short by that old adventure, unable to act, unable to confess. Then the feelings of guilt began, the regret and the grief. Sometimes he could choke them down, but at other times they overcame him – until the day of his wedding when a gypsy's cry from the pine trees dramatically reminded him of his solemn oath.

In this same journal, he scratched several more words in haste, at dawn, before leaving Yvonne de Galais, his wife from the previous evening – leaving with her permission, but for ever.

> I must go. I must find the tracks left by the two gypsies who came to the forest today and departed on their bicycles, going east. I will return to Yvonne only after I have made sure that Frantz and Valentine are married and installed in his house.
>
> This manuscript, which I started as a secret diary and which has served as my confession, will be the property of my friend François Seurel if I do not return.

In haste, he must have slipped the notebook under others in his old school trunk, turned the key, and vanished.

TIME passed. I lost hope of ever seeing Meaulnes again. Dismal days creaked by in the country school, miserable days in the empty house. Frantz did not keep the appointment I had arranged. On top of everything, Aunt Moinel had no idea where Valentine was living.

The only source of joy at Les Sablonnières was the little girl whose life had been saved. By the end of September, she had turned into a bouncing, pretty baby, about to celebrate her first birthday. She would push a chair along, hanging on to its rungs, trying to walk by herself without fear of falling, and making a reverberating racket throughout the abandoned house. When I held her in my arms, she never let me kiss her but, wild and flirtatious at the same time, would wriggle and push my face away with her tiny open palm, bursting with laughter. With her gaiety and ferocity, she chased away the sorrows that had weighed down the house since her birth. I sometimes said to myself that in spite of her wildness, she would – somehow – become my child. But once again, Providence had other ideas.

One Sunday morning at the end of September, I got up very early, even before the countrywoman who looked after the little girl. I had made plans to go fishing on the Cher with Jasmin Delouche and two men from Saint-Benoist. The local villagers often invited me along on poaching parties, fishing with nets, which was forbidden, or by hand. All during the summer, on our days off, we would set out at dawn and not return until noon. It was a paying job for most of these men, but for me it was my only pastime, the only exploit reminding me of my previous escapades. I began to get a taste for these excursions, these long fishing expeditions along the river or among the reeds in the pond.

That morning, I was already up at half past five, waiting in front of the house, under a lean-to against the wall separating the formal garden at Les Sablonnières from the vegetable garden at the farm. I was busy untangling my nets which I had thrown down in a heap the previous Thursday.

It wasn't quite day. It was the half-light of a beautiful September morning, and the shed where I was hurriedly unravelling the nets was still plunged in shadow. I was working silently and busily, when suddenly I heard the gate open, and footsteps crunching on the gravel.

'Uh-oh!' I said to myself. 'They're even earlier than I expected. I'm not ready yet.'

But the man who came into the courtyard did not look familiar. As far as I could distinguish, he was a tall, strapping, bearded fellow, dressed like a hunter or a poacher. He went straight to the front door, instead of coming to find me and the others in the usual meeting place.

'Good,' I thought. 'It is one of their friends they invited without telling me. They've sent him along as a scout.'

The man fiddled cautiously with the door latch. But I had locked it behind me when I came out. He did the same with the kitchen entry. Then, pausing for an instant, he turned towards me, and his anxious face was illumined by the brightening day. Only then did I recognise Meaulnes.

I stood there for a long time, scared, desperate, and suddenly overwhelmed by the sadness his return stirred up. He disappeared behind the house, made a complete tour, and came back, hesitating.

Then I advanced towards him and, without a word, hugged him, sobbing. He understood at once.

'She's dead, isn't she?' he said in a clipped voice.

He stood there, silent, still, and terrifying. I took him by the hand

and led him gently towards the house. Day had broken by then. I wanted to get the worst over as quickly as possible, so I made him climb the stairs which led towards Yvonne's room. As soon as he entered, he fell on his knees in front of her bed, and remained there for a long time with his head enfolded in his two arms.

Eventually he got up, his eyes distraught, and staggered around, unaware of where he was. Then, still guiding him by the arm, I opened the door which communicated with the baby's room. Her nurse was downstairs, but she was already awake, resolutely sitting up in her cradle. All we could see of her was her head turned towards us in astonishment.

'Here is your daughter,' I said.

He gave a start and looked at me.

Then he seized her and lifted her up in his arms. He could not see her very well at first because he was crying so hard. To divert attention from his emotion and flood of tears, but still holding her close to him with his right arm, he lowered his head to me and said:

'I have brought them back, the two others. You can visit them in their house.' (And in fact, later that same morning I set off, wrapped in thought and almost happy, for Frantz's house, the deserted cottage Yvonne de Galais had shown me. As I approached, I saw from a distance the perfect example of a young housewife wearing a lace collar, sweeping her doorstep, much to the curious admiration of several young cowherds in their Sunday best, on their way to Mass.)

Meanwhile, the baby became bored with being held so tightly. As Augustin continued not to look at her, keeping his head lowered to one side to staunch his tears, she gave him a sharp clout on his damp, bearded mouth with her tiny hand.

That attracted his attention at last, and he threw her up in the air and caught her, gazing at her with a sort of laugh. She clapped her hands in glee.

I drew back so that I could see them better. Downhearted, but filled with wonder all the same, I was sure the child had at last found the companion she unconsciously awaited. Meaulnes had returned to take away my last remaining joy, and I could already imagine him gathering his daughter under his cloak and setting off that very night for new adventures.

THE HISTORY OF VINTAGE

The famous American publisher Alfred A. Knopf (1892–1984) founded Vintage Books in the United States in 1954 as a paperback home for the authors published by his company. Vintage was launched in the United Kingdom in 1990 and works independently from the American imprint although both are part of the international publishing group, Random House.

Vintage in the United Kingdom was initially created to publish paperback editions of books acquired by the prestigious hardback imprints in the Random House Group such as Jonathan Cape, Chatto & Windus, Hutchinson and later William Heinemann, Secker & Warburg and The Harvill Press. There are many Booker and Nobel Prize-winning authors on the Vintage list and the imprint publishes a huge variety of fiction and non-fiction. Over the years Vintage has expanded and the list now includes great authors of the past – who are published under the Vintage Classics imprint – as well as many of the most influential authors of the present.

For a full list of the books Vintage publishes, please visit our website
www.vintage-books.co.uk

For book details and other information about the classic authors we publish, please visit the Vintage Classics website
www.vintage-classics.info

www.vintage-classics.info